E. NESBIT FAIRY STORIES

'The stories in the present book are a choice
from E. Nesbit's separate shorter tales with
a magical content. In each you hear the
unmistakable Nesbit voice from the start;
easy, zestful, sure, audacious, with a running
current of humour, the friendly
conspiratorial voice of a storyteller who is
clearly addressing the reader personally.
'As we read the stories here, with their high
spirits, their reckless pace and their still
more reckless invention, we are again and
again reminded of that special feature of
Nesbit-country, no matter what book or tale
we enter it by: the nearness of magic to
everyday life; the nearness to daily life of
the wildest fantasy. Imagination is the one
true link. Meanwhile, the very verve and
impulsiveness of these tales brings us
uncannily close to the writer at work . . . E.
Nesbit lives, and her world goes on so long
as her books are read. This could be a long
time yet.'

from the introduction by
Naomi Lewis

E. NESBIT FAIRY STORIES

'Naomi Lewis would, I think, be
the first to agree that E. Nesbit's
fairy stories, with their special
flavour of everyday take-it-or-leave-
it magic, draw children in. The lucid,
perceptive and witty introduction
and the notes which relate the
stories to the life of the author are
for the delight of older Nesbit
admirers. Brian Robb's half-magic
line illustrations are the perfect
complement for these tales.'

Elaine Moss,
Children's Books of the Year

E. Nesbit Fairy Stories

Edited by Naomi Lewis

Illustrated by Brian Robb

SCHOLASTIC PUBLICATIONS LIMITED
by arrangement with
Hodder & Stoughton

First published 1977 by Ernest Benn Limited

Knight Books edition 1979 (shortened to exclude the
stories '*Billy and William*' and '*The Last of the Dragons*')
Second impression, 1980

Reproduced, printed and bound in Great Britain for
Hodder and Stoughton Paperbacks a
division of Hodder and Stoughton Ltd.,
Mill Road, Dunton Green, Sevenoaks,
Kent (Editorial Office: 47 Bedford
Square, London WC1 3DP) by
Cox & Wyman Ltd, Reading

ISBN 0 340 25537 4

Contents

Foreword by NAOMI LEWIS   i
    [Introductory notes to the stories are also by
    NAOMI LEWIS]

Billy the King   ix

The Charmed Life or the Princess and the
    Lift-man   23

Melisande or Long and Short Division   43

The Town in the Library in the Town in the
    Library   65

Belinda and Bellamant or the Bells of Carillon-
    Land   85

The White Horse   109

Fortunatus Rex & Co. or the Mystery of the
    Disappearing Schoolgirls   125

Foreword by Naomi Lewis

In 1899 the first of countless thousands of children had the luck to open a book and read these inviting words:

> This is the story of the different ways we looked for treasure, and I think when you have read it you will see that we were not lazy about the looking.
>
> There are some things I must tell before I begin to tell about the treasure-seeking, because I have read books myself, and I know how beastly it is when a story begins, 'Alas!' said Hildegarde with a deep sigh, 'we must look our last on this ancestral home,' —and then someone else says something—and you don't know for pages and pages where the home is, or who Hildegarde is, or anything about it. Our ancestral home is in the Lewisham Road. It is semi-detached. There are six of us besides Father . . .

The Bastables had arrived!—and so, in a special sense, had their author. Thereafter, like a new voice for the new century, she was to produce a further seventeen books, all of them eagerly seized on in her day, and still devotedly read. 'Her books,' wrote one enthusiast, 'have meant a very great deal to me, not only while I was a little boy of nine and upwards, but right up to the present day. I have re-read them each at least twenty times. She had an economy of phrase, and an unparalleled talent for evoking hot summer days in the English countryside.' This reader was Noel Coward.

But who *was* Hildegarde? Or rather—for this is what concerns us now —who was E. Nesbit? The answer is both a portrait and a story.

Anyone who sets out to write the first biography of someone no longer living has the problems of the detective, of the explorer in unmapped country and—especially—of the archaeologist. Clues disappear like snow, never to come again. Essential papers may have been deliberately burnt, or lost; humans take their memories when they go. However, two pieces of good fortune have made E. Nesbit very much more than a name on a printed page. First, her biographer Doris Langley Moore began her quest (like Mrs Gaskell) only a few years after her subject's death, when numerous first-hand witnesses were alive. She caught them just in time. Thirty or so years later, when the biography was revised, not one of these contributors remained. The second—which gave the key to the one locked door, the years of childhood—was the discovery of a series of autobiographical articles by E. Nesbit in the files of the long-dead *Girl's Own Paper*. How and why these reminiscences came to be written, what part they played in transforming their author into Nesbit the master storyteller —these things belong to the tale that follows.

E. Nesbit—known in her home as Daisy—was born 15 August, 1858, in South-East London, the youngest of five surviving children. Saretta her half-sister was 14 when she was born; Mary 6, Alfred 4 and Henry 3 Her father, an extremely gifted man with a wide reputation as an agricultural scientist, was at this time owner and principal of a Chemical and Agricultural College in Kennington, and here the family lived. Sadly, her father died when Daisy was not quite four. Mrs Nesbit, a courageous and enterprising character, took over the running of the college; but three years later a new trouble changed all plans. Mary's fragile health was causing alarm.

Consumption, the old, rather terrible name for tuberculosis, is today no longer a dangerous matter. But in the 19th century and even into our own, it was the greatest of destroyers, especially of quite young people. Among its best-known victims were Keats and his brother, the Brontës, Chopin, Katherine Mansfield—the list is endless. The boys and Daisy were sent away to schools; the older girls and the mother moved to France. Mrs Nesbit went to Daisy's school to say goodbye, but the little girl put up so intense a resistance to being left behind that she was taken too. And so began her Continental travels described in the *Girl's Own Paper* reminiscences. Sometimes she was with her mother and sisters; sometimes she was left with a family, or in a school. 'It is a mistake,' she noted very long afterwards, 'to suppose that children are naturally fond of change. They love what they know ... they want to get back to the house they know, the toys they know, the books they know.' But where *was* this sure base? 'Home' changed, and changed.

Yet there were bright passages—one in particular when a house was taken in Dinan, Brittany, from July 1868 until early in 1870. In the reminiscences she recalls the immense walled fruit garden, the swing in the cherry orchard, the little black cow and pig and goat, the ponies, Punch and Judy. A tiny footnote to history is the fact that Mrs Nesbit let this house to the Kitchener family in the summer of 1869. The future Lord Kitchener, then about 18, rode Daisy's pony carelessly and made it lame. She held this against him always.

But when is history separate from our lives? It was the Franco-Prussian War in 1870 (Daisy was then at school in Germany) that brought the Nesbits back to England. Here, Mary, now 18 became engaged to a young Pre-Raphaelite poet, the blind Philip Marston (1850–87). You can find two poems of his in the Oxford Book of Victorian Verse. As a result, Daisy at 12 or so had the chance of meeting such legendary characters as Rossetti, Morris, Swinburne and Burne-Jones, especially when the two girls went to stay for a while with Christina Rossetti, and her mother. (Was it here that they took part in a strenuous game of hide-and-seek with Dante Gabriel?) E. Nesbit's taste, in adult life, for loose flowing clothes in 'artistic' colours—the kind of dress that Mrs Morris and other lovely Pre-Raphaelite ladies would have been wearing—may well have had its origin in this period. Meanwhile, among all these poets and painters, Daisy was not idle. Always a busy writer of verse, she even tried her hand at that favourite Pre-Raphaelite form, a sonnet—'To My Sister's Portrait'. Here are its open and closing lines.

It is so lovely! Yet that portrait shews
But one half of her beauty, auburn hair
Falls o'er her shoulders and her throat, small fair
Soft hands, and a delicate Grecian nose! . . .

Some love thee sadly without hope of love,
Some give thee love while hoping for the same,
Some love thee with a love that cannot die
And, Maris Stella, such a one am I.

Which Pre-Raphaelite painted the portrait? What became of it? But Mary, the 'Maris Stella', had little more time. She died at the age of 20, after a final unavailing journey to France.

And now Mrs Nesbit (from whom her daughter must have learnt much that she would need when facing blows in later life) looked for a country house where the family could settle at last. She found one, Halstead Hall, in Kent; it would always remain the best-loved of Daisy's homes. 'There never were such peonies as grew among our currant-bushes, not such apricots as hung among the leaves on the sunny south wall.' There was a pond (with a raft) surrounded by clustering lilac bushes; there was a secret enclosure on the roof where she and Alfred and Henry kept a store of books and had picnics of tinned pineapple. House and garden would live again in the Nesbit stories, so would a nearby railway cutting, part of the Knockholt line, another favourite haunt of the dauntless trio. When the boys were away at school Daisy would hide among the lilacs, dreamily reading Mrs Ewing; or she would sit at the window of her own room, looking out on the rich summer trees and flowers, and there she would write—'verse, verse, always verse—and dream of the days when I should be a great poet like Shakespeare, or Christina Rossetti . . . I never doubted then that it would come.'

But after about three years, this shining chapter also came to an end. Mrs Nesbit's money was gone. They moved to London, near the Angel, Islington, a part which always appears in E. Nesbit's books as a poor, depressing place [see note to 'King Billy']. Still, Daisy was a lively and pretty girl; we hear of friends, of roller-skating, of the occasional beau. But only one thing is of importance. It was in London that she met, and presently married, Hubert Bland. He was 25, she 22.

Photographs of Bland in middle life show him as strongly built, dandy-ish, with a narrow moustache, determined mouth, and a monocle worn on a black ribbon; the whole effect is oddly formidable. At the time of the wedding (1880) he had much the same personality, but he still had no idea where his real abilities lay. The marriage (1880) started with crisis and near-disaster—a pattern that would recur in various forms over the years. Bland caught smallpox; his partner in an unlikely business venture absconded with the funds, and Edith, now with a very young baby, Paul, had to find a rapid way of earning the family's living. She painted greetings cards, gave recitations at private concerts (these were days before radio, television, cinema, or recorded music); she scribbled away at articles, verses and stories, hawking them round 'in a black dress, pale as a ghost, shivering with cold, and altogether wearing a look of distress' as one description runs.

Bland slowly recovered and began to discover his gift for political journalism and lecturing. Edith continued to write and sell her verse and stories. They were a striking pair. Both had exceptional looks and charm; both had the power of attracting friends of high mental calibre. Their home (or homes; there were several moves) became a centre for young progressive writers and thinkers—young Shaw and young Wells, for instance. A second child, Iris, had arrived; there would be a third, Fabian, in 1885. A young woman, Alice Hoatson, who was working in a magazine when the ghostlike Edith brought round a manuscript, remained an admiring friend, and before long, left her job to join the attractive bohemian household, with its poverty and excitements, as a sort of general *aide*. The Blands were founder-members of the Fabian Society; Hubert was in the Chair at the Founding Meeting in January 1884. The Society—a discussion centre for intellectual Socialists before a Socialist party existed in this country—drew in some remarkable characters: Havelock Ellis, Mrs Besant, Charles Bradlaugh, Shaw and Wells, even Frederick ('Corvo') Rolfe.

One of the many descriptions of Edith at this period comes from the recollections of the writer Richard Le Gallienne; then about 23, she some eight years older.

> I looked on her with wonder, captivated by her beauty and the charm of her immediately sympathetic response. I fell head over ears in love with her, in fact. She was quite unlike any woman I had ever seen, with her tall, lithe, boyish-girl figure admirably set off by her plain 'socialist' gown, her short hair, and her large vivid eyes, curiously bird-like, and so full of intelligence and a certain half-mocking, yet friendly humour. She had, too, a comradely frankness of manner, which made me at once feel that I had known her all my life; like a tom-boyish sister slightly older than myself. She suggested adventure, playing truant, robbing orchards, or even running away to sea. I was hers from that moment, and have been hers ever since.

She never at any time lacked admirers and followers. But there *are* clues here to why she usually writes from the boy's view in her children's books. For one thing she had little patience with the tame and empty lives of so many girls and married women. Her own mother had been no cipher; she in turn had to take on every kind of responsibility, earning much of the family income. Besides, both as child and adult she loved what might then be seen as boys' activities. And, in thoroughly modern fashion, she sang spirited songs to her own guitar.

The Blands were impressive, too, as hosts. When funds were low, the main dish might be no more than beans, elegantly served from a huge tureen. Yet the cloth and silver and candles and roses (from the garden) gave the table the air of a banquet—and the guests and the conversation had, from reports, an almost legendary quality.

But there were troubles as well. Hubert Bland had never been able to resist attracting women, and the effects of his many affairs could not leave Edith undisturbed. And then, soon after Fabian was born, Miss Hoatson gave birth to a child. Illegitimacy was thought a great disgrace, and Edith promised to adopt the infant (Rosamund) as one of the family. She kept this promise, but it was a shock to find that Hubert was the father. Perhaps it is not surprising to find that Bland was unusually strict with his own two daughters. He even managed to pass on his dislike of the Suffragettes to Edith herself. That reactionary stance was the cause of a break with one of their best friends, the writer Laurence Housman.

But now, when E. Nesbit was nearing 40, a strange, almost magical transformation came about; the busy author for adults, suddenly became another, the unique E. Nesbit who opened new paths in children's fiction. What had happened? An invitation had come from the *Girl's Own Paper* to write a piece on her schooldays. It arrived at a time of restlessness and low spirits. She began to think of her childhood, and the single essay developed into a number of chapters, running in the paper from October 1896 to September 1897. Her imagination was fired; she began *The Treasure Seekers*.

The other books followed fast; they brought fame, and praise—and money. In 1899 the Blands made their final move—to Well Hall, in Eltham, Kent, a large old rambling mansion with an ancient moat in its grounds. But disaster matched the luck. In 1899 Edith gave birth to another child, who died. A second child (John)—Bland's and Miss Hoatson's—was born a few months later; like Rosamund, this infant had to be taken in and brought up as her own. (Miss Hoatson seems to have been oddly detached about these young; her real attachment was always to the adult Blands.) And then, in October 1900, Fabian, now 15, the boy who seemed to E. Nesbit most like herself, died during a minor operation from the medical incompetence of the time.

Do we find any trace of all this in the stories? No, indeed—for in these, she steps completely back into the sunlit world of the best time in her past. Except in *The Enchanted Castle*, she rejected all the memories that held fear (and there are plenty of these in the reminiscences); she did not wish any child, she said, to feel the many terrors that she had felt.

E. Nesbit lived until 1924. Bland had died 10 years earlier, after a long illness, and the 1914 war brought other changes and griefs. But it is good to know that the tide of happiness turned for her again. She married an ex-sea-captain, Thomas Tucker, lively, kind and devoted. They settled in a boat-like home near Dymchurch, living in the sort of way, in the sort of place, that the Bastables might have invented for their author's final days.

The stories in the present book are a choice from E. Nesbit's separate shorter tales with a magical content. The triumphant reception of the Bastable and Psammead books led to a continual demand for her work in the *Strand* and other leading magazines, before being published in book form. This is where nearly all of the tales here were originally read—by adults as well as by their juniors. In each you hear the unmistakeable Nesbit voice from the start, easy, zestful, sure, audacious, with a running current of humour, the friendly conspiratorial voice of a storyteller who is clearly addressing the reader personally. You can also tell that she was a rapid spontaneous writer, sped on by her fertile thoughts, not often pausing to read again.

During the 1890s the Fairy Books of Andrew Lang—the Blue, the Red and the rest—had brought the traditional fairy tales handsomely back into fashion. What E. Nesbit did was to impose their pattern on everyday modern life, with its lifts (very new at the turn of the century), its railways, bicycles, its Lee-Mitford rifle, its new play *Candida* by Shaw, its mail-order catalogue, where a prince might seek a spouse:

Prince Bellamant, aged twenty-four. Wants Princess who doesn't object to a christening curse. Nature of curse only revealed in the strictess confidence. Good-tempered. Comfortably off. No relations.

its speculative builders, even then destroying the countryside. 'It is curious,' she notes, 'that nearly all the great fortunes are made by turning beautiful things into ugly ones. Making beauty out of ugliness is very ill-paid work.' She might be writing now.

One of the stories here should have a particular interest for Nesbit-followers. This is 'The Town in the Library' probably the earliest of all in date, indeed, it would be hard to find any other that is so directly personal. It takes us right into the house where she was writing; its two main characters, Fabian and Rosamund, were real Bland children; the toys were their own toys. And the whole thing is based on a special Nesbit game or invention—the building of miniature towns and scenes from wooden bricks and books and chessmen and candlesticks and pieces of mirror—any item to hand. It stayed and grew for years, both in fact and imagination, until it took permanent form in one of the last of her full-length books, that strange, uneven, haunting tale *The Magic City* (1910). One of its child readers was C. S. Lewis; and echoes clearly remained in his mind when he came to write the Narnia stories.

Still to her Edwardian readers, the most entertaining of all her notions must surely have been her showing of Kings and Queens as mere sub-urban persons, or as applying for jobs (in their own trade, to be sure) at common employment agencies. ('Good steady King wanted. Must be quick, willing and up to his work.') All this was a tremendous joke at a time when Europe—perhaps for the last time in history—was full of ruling monarchs and royal courts not unlike those of a fairy tale.

But there are few signs of Fabian Socialism in her work. There is, to be sure, a Utopian scene in *The Amulet*, inspired partly by Wells (who gets a flattering mention), partly by William Morris; but this is a conscious setpiece. Perhaps we ought to recall, too, when Father, in *The Railway Children* (1905) is accused of selling secrets to Russia, that this would be *Czarist* Russia, and that the gentle Anarchist Prince Kropotkin (who, by the way, taught little Arthur Ransome to skate) was one of the Blands' warm friends. Essentially, though, she wrote of the middle-class scene she knew, with all its accepted attitudes. She was a rebel herself in many things, but the rebellion concerned her own life, not the world. She worked hard to organize treats for the poor of Deptford; but it is the same poor, not quite so humble, now become servants, errand-boys, cooks, who are the vulgar comics in her tales. As for that sensitive slum-boy, little Dick Harding, is he not really titled Richard Arden, lost heir to an ancient line?

And yet, in spite of all provisos, the Nesbit books stay obstinately alive. And if we ask *Why*? we do find certain clues. For one thing, as with all great writers for the young, she did not write 'down' to children, nor at, nor for them exactly. She really wrote for and about the child who had been herself. As with Carroll, Andersen, Masefield, Stevenson, Tolkein, the Dickens of *David Copperfield*, a streak of childhood, undissolved, stayed with her to the end of her writing life. 'There is only one way of understanding children,' she noted; 'they cannot be understood by imagination, or observation, nor even by love. They can only be understood by memory . . . The reason why those children are like real children is that I was a child once myself, and by some fortunate chance I remember exactly how I used to feel and think about things.' So, in her books, she was able to see behaviour, however outrageous, entirely from the view of the young—a considerable adult feat.

This is not all. Running through all her best and most characteristic work is an abiding sense of comedy, spirited and resilient, hard to define, very hard indeed to reproduce. It can be found at its dazzling best in the first two Bastable books, where a phrase as well as an episode can still stir a reader into wild and helpless laughter. 'Any success my stories have had is due, I think, to a sort of light-hearted outlook on life,' she wrote to Lady Dunsany. The other factor is what might be called the personal voice, the product of whatever is stored in the writer's mind from experiences, from seeing and listening,—and from reading other books. You can sense this personal voice on every page.

Most of the children in Nesbit tales are themselves addicted readers; books are the basis of their exploits and schemes and dreams, sometimes their language too. Anyone with a taste for sleuthing can track down some of the books that fertilised E. Nesbit's imagination: Kenneth Grahame's *The Golden Age* and *Dream Days*, F. Anstey's *The Brass Bottle*, George MacDonald's *The Princess and the Goblin*, *The Light Princess* and *Sir Gibbie*, Dickens's *Holiday Romance*, the *Alice* books for sure. What later writers owe to E. Nesbit herself—often unconsciously—can scarcely be calculated.

There is, indeed, less difference between the 'magic' and 'non-magic' Nesbit books than one would think. In the Bastable tales, in *The Railway Children*, even, the theme is very much like that of the Psammead saga— the pursuing (with many a trial and error) of the idea of the wish. It was a matter that E. Nesbit, like the ancient storytellers, understood thoroughly. Her stories never fail to show the great truths about magic: that every wish has its price, that even magic itself wears thin with too much use, that if you haven't much imagination you won't get much of a wish! Glance, say, at *Five Children and It*:

> 'We want,' said Robert slowly, 'to be rich beyond the dreams of something or other.'
>
> 'Avarice,' said Jane.
>
> 'So it is,' said the Fairy unexpectedly. 'But it won't do you much good, that's one comfort,' it muttered to itself. 'Come—I can't go beyond dreams, you know! How much do you want, and will you have it in gold or notes?'
>
> 'Gold, please—and millions of it.'
>
> 'This gravel-pit be full enough?' said the Fairy in an offhand manner . . .

Well, we all know what happened after that.

And as we read the stories here, with their high spirits, their reckless pace and still more reckless invention, we are again and again reminded of that special feature of Nesbit-country, no matter what book or tale we enter it by: the nearness of magic to everyday life; the nearness to daily life of the wildest fantasy. Imagination is the one true link. Meanwhile, the very verve and impulsiveness of these tales bring us uncannily close to the writer herself at work: thoughts of past and present, of Claremont Square, Islington, and of the waiting Kentish coast; ordinary objects at hand—a catalogue, a kite, a saucepan of homemade toffee like brown glass (surely you could skate on it!)—all of these, as her pen dashes on, become matter of fairy tale. And here before us these objects are today absolutely unchanged, whatever may have happened to them in fact. 'Can a cricket bat disappear?' asks Arthur Waley in a poem about the things he owned as a boy, long ago. Can a sled called Rosebud vanish entirely?—such was the secret question of *Citizen Kane*. Each question is an answer in itself. This is surely what Mr Noah means in the *Magic City*, when he says to Philip: 'It's a little difficult, I own. But you see, you built those cities in two worlds. It's pulled down in this world. But in the other world it's going on'. E. Nesbit lives, and her world goes on so long as her books are read. This could be a long time yet.

Billy the King

Billy the King

The splendid opening of this story—the Registry Office with jobs for kings and queens ('Good steady King wanted. Must be quick, willing, and up to his work')—has the mark of true Nesbit. As you will see from most of the stories here, she believed in linking everyday life with the ancient magic of fairy tale. In her own time employment offices for servants were extremely busy, and phrased their advertisements for cooks and kitchenmaids in just this peremptory way. So the episode, applied to kings and queens, was indeed a saucy one. (See, too, the note on *A Charmed Life*.) The pig and the lizard could be second cousins to those in *Alice*; but the sea of treacle, made swimmable-in by the dragon's warmth, then hardening into toffee for skating over, is a stunning piece of Nesbit invention. It must be said that, by today's standards, she is rather hard on Claremont Square, which is a quiet square of terraced houses set on a hill not far from the Angel, Islington—but there *is* a probable reason for her dislike. When she was in her later teens in the 1870s, the Nesbit family became very poor and moved from their loved house and garden in Halstead, Kent (scene of the Bastable tales) to this part of London. So it stood, for her, as a place of poverty, drabness and loss.

N.L.

'NOW, WILLIAM,' said Billy King's great-uncle, 'you are old enough to earn your own living, so I shall find you a nice situation in an office, and you will not return to school.'

The blood of Billy King ran cold in his veins. He looked out over the brown wire blinds into Claremont Square, Pentonville, which was where his uncle lived and the tears came into his eyes; for, though his uncle thought he was old enough to earn his own living, he was still young enough to hate the idea of having to earn it in an office, where he would never do anything, or make anything, or see anything, but only add up dull figures from year's end to year's end.

'I don't care,' said Billy to himself. 'I'll run away and get a situation on my own—something interesting. I wonder if I could learn how to be a pirate captain or a highwayman?'

And next morning Billy got up very early, before anyone was about, and ran away.

He ran till he was out of breath and then he walked, and he walked till he was out of patience, and then he ran again, and between walking and running he came at last plump up to the door of a shop. And over the shop there were big painted letters saying, 'Registry office for all sorts of persons out of employment.'

'I'm out of employment, anyway,' said he. The window of the shop had big green-baize-shutter sort of things in it, with white cards fastened on to them with drawing-pins, and on the cards were written the kind of persons out of employment the registry office had got places for. And in the very first one he read there was his own name—King!

'I've come to the right shop,' said Billy, and he read the card through. 'Good general King wanted. Must be used to the business.'

'That's not me, I'm afraid,' thought Billy, 'because whatever a general King's business is, I can't be used to it till I've tried it.'

The next was: 'Good steady King wanted. Must be quick, willing, and up to his work.'

'I'm willing enough,' said Billy, 'and I'm quick enough —at any rate, at fives or footer—but I don't know what a steady King's work is.' So he looked at another card.

'Wanted, respectable King to take entire charge of Parliament, and to assist in Cabinet Councils and Reform of the Army, to open Bazaars and Schools of Art, and make himself generally useful.'

Billy shook his head.

'I think that must be a very hard place,' said he.

The next was: 'Competent Queen wanted; economical and good manager.'

'Whatever else I am I'm not a Queen,' said Billy, and he was just turning sadly away, when he saw a little card

2

stuck away in the right-hand top corner of the baize field.

'Hard-working King wanted; no objection to one who has not been out before.'

'I can but try,' said Billy, and he opened the door of the registry office and walked in.

Inside there were several desks. At the first desk a lion with a pen behind its ear was dictating to a unicorn, who was writing in a series of blue books with his horn. Billy noticed that the horn had been sharpened to a nice point, like a lead pencil when the drawing-master does it for you as a favour.

'I think you want a King?' said Billy timidly.

'No, we don't,' said the lion, and it turned on him so quickly that Billy was sorry he had spoken. 'The situation is filled, young man, and we're thoroughly suited.'

Billy was turning away, much dispirited, when the unicorn said: 'Try some of the others.'

So he went on to the next desk, where a frog sat sadly. But it only wanted Presidents; and at the next desk an eagle told him that only Emperors were wanted, and those very seldom. It was not till he got to the very end of the long room that Billy found a desk where a fat pig in spectacles sat reading a cookery-book.

'Do you want a King?' said Billy. 'I've not been out before.'

'Then you're the King for us,' said the pig, shutting the cookery-book with a bang. 'Hard-working, I suppose, as the notice says?'

'I think I should be,' said Billy, adding, honestly, 'especially if I liked the work.'

The pig gave him a square of silver parchment and said, 'That's the address.'

On the parchment was written:

'Kingdom of Plurimiregia. Billy King, Respectable Monarch. Not been out before.'

'You'd better go by post,' said the pig. 'The five o'clock post will do.'

'But why—but how—where is it?' asked Billy.

'I don't know where it is,' said the pig, 'but the Post Office knows everything. As to how—why, you just a tie a label round your neck and post yourself in the nearest letter-box. As to why, that's a silly question, really, your Majesty. Don't you know the Post Office always takes charge of the Royal males?'

Billy was just putting the address carefully away in what would have been his watch-pocket if he had had any relation in the world except a great-uncle, when the swing door opened gently and a little girl came in. She looked at the lion and unicorn and the other busy beasts behind their desks, and she did not seem to like the look of them. She looked up the long room and saw Billy, and she came straight up to him and said:

'Please I want a situation as Queen. It says in the window previous experience not required.'

She was a very shabby little girl, with a clean, round,

rosy face, and she looked as little like a Queen with previous experience as anybody could possibly have done.

'I'm not the registry office, my good kid,' said Billy.

And the pig said, 'Try the next desk.'

Behind the next desk sat a lizard, but it was so large it was more like an alligator, only with a less unpleasant expression about the mouth.

'Speak to him,' said the pig, as the lizard leaned forward on his front paws like a draper's assistant when he says, 'What's the next article?'

'I don't like to,' said the little girl.

'Nonsense, you little duffer!' said Billy kindly; 'he won't eat you.'

'Are you sure?' said the little girl very earnestly.

Then Billy said, 'Look here, I'm a King, and so I've got a situation. Are you a Queen?'

'My name's Eliza MacQueen,' said the little girl. 'I suppose that's near enough.'

'Well, then,' said Billy to the lizard, 'will she do?'

'Perfectly, I should say,' replied the lizard, with a smile that did not become him very well. 'Here is the address.' He gave it to her; it read:

'Kingdom of Allexanassa. Queen, not been out before; willing, obliging, and anxious to learn.'

'Your kingdoms,' he added, 'are next door to each other.'

'So we shall see each other often,' said Billy. 'Cheer up! We might travel together, perhaps.'

'No,' said the pig; 'Queens go by railway. A Queen has to begin to get used to her train as soon as she can. Now, run along, do. My friend here will see her off.'

'You're sure they won't eat me?' said Eliza—and Billy was certain they wouldn't though he didn't know why. So he said, 'Good-bye. I hope you'll get on in your new place,' and off he went to buy a penny luggage label at the expensive stationer's three doors down the street on the right-hand side. And when he had addressed the label and tied it round his neck, he posted himself honourably at the General Post Office. The rest of the letters in the box made a fairly comfortable bed, and Billy fell asleep. When he awoke he was being delivered by the early morning postman at the Houses of Parliament in the capital of Plurimiregia, and the Houses of Parliament were just being opened for the day. The air of Plurimiregia was clear and blue, very different from the air of Claremont Square, Pentonville. The hills and woods round the town looked soft and green from the hill in the middle of the town where the Parliament Houses stood. The town itself was small and very pretty, like one of the towns in old illuminated books, and it had a great wall all round it, and orange-trees growing on the wall. Billy wondered whether it was forbidden to pick the oranges.

When Parliament was opened by the footman whose business it was, Billy said:

'Please, I've come about the place——'

'The King's or the cook's?' asked the footman.

Billy was rather angry.

'Now, do I look like a cook?, he said.

'The question is, do you look like a King?' said the footman.

'If I get the place you will be sorry for this,' said Billy.

'If you get the place you won't keep it long,' said the footman. 'It's not worth while being disagreeable; there's not time to do it properly in. Come along in.'

Billy went along in, and the footman led him into the presence of the Prime Minister, who was sitting with straws in his hair, wringing his hands.

'Come by post, your lordship,' the footman said—'from London.'

The Prime Minister left off wringing his hands, and held one of them out to Billy. 'You will suit!' he said. 'I'll engage you in a minute. But just pull the straws out of my hair first, will you? I only put them in because we hadn't been able to find a suitable King, and I find straws so useful in helping my brain to act in a crisis. Of course, once you're engaged for the situation, no one will ask you to do anything useful.'

Billy pulled the straws out, and the Prime Minister said:

'Are they all out? Thanks. Well, now you're engaged—
six months on trial. You needn't do anything you don't
want to. Now, your Majesty, breakfast is served at nine.
Let me conduct you to the Royal apartments.'

In ten minutes Billy had come out of a silver bath filled
with scented water, and was putting on the grandest
clothes he had ever seen in his life.

For the first time in his life it was with personal
pleasure, and not from a sense of duty, that he brushed his
hair and satisfied himself that none of his nails was in
mourning. Then he went to breakfast, which was so
fine that none but a French cook could have either cooked
or described it. He was a little hungry—he had had
nothing to eat since the bread and cheese at supper in
Claremont Square the night before last.

After breakfast he rode out on a white pony, a thing he
might have lived in Claremont Square for ever without
doing. And he found he rode very well. After the ride he
went on the sea in a boat, and was surprised and delighted
to find that he knew how to sail as well as how to steer. In
the afternoon he was taken to a circus; and in the evening
the whole Court played blind-man's buff. A most enchant-
ing day!

Next morning the breakfast was boiled, underdone eggs
and burnt herrings. The King was too polite to make
remarks about his food, but he did feel a little disappointed.

The Prime Minister was late for breakfast and came in

looking hot and flurried, and a garland of straw was entwined in the Prime Ministerial hair.

'Excuse my hair, Sire,' he said. 'The cook left last night, but a new one comes at noon to-day. Meantime, I have done my best.'

Billy said it was all right, and he had had an excellent breakfast. The second day passed as happily as the first; the cook seemed to have arrived, for the breakfast was made up for by the lunch. And Billy had the pleasure of shooting at a target at two thousand yards with the Lee-Metford rifle which had arrived by the same post as himself, and hitting the bull's-eye every time.

This is really a rare thing—even when you are a King. But Billy began to think it curious that he should never have found out before how clever he was, and when he took down a volume of Virgil and found that he could read it as easily as though it had been *The Child's First Reading-Book*, he was really astonished. So Billy said to the Prime Minister:

'How is it I know so many things without learning them?'

'It's the rule here, Sire,' said the Prime Minister. 'Kings are allowed to know everything without learning it.'

Now, the next morning Billy woke very early and got up and went out into the garden, and, turning a corner suddenly, he came upon a little person in a large white cap, with a large apron on in which she was gathering sweet potherbs, thyme, and basil, and mint, and savory, and sage, and marjoram. She stood up and dropped a curtsy.

'Halloa!' said Billy the King; 'who are you?'

'I'm the new cook,' said the person in the apron.

Her big flapping cap hid her face, but Billy knew her voice.

'Why,' said he, turning her face up with his hands under her chin, 'you're Eliza!'

And sure enough it was Eliza, but her round face looked very much cleverer and prettier than it had done when he saw it last.

'Hush!' she said. 'Yes, I am. I got the place as Queen of Allexanassa, but it was all horribly grand, and such long trains, and the crown is awfully heavy. And yesterday morning I woke very early, and I thought I'd just put on my old frock, and I went out, and there was a man with a boat, and he didn't know I was the Queen, and I got him to take me for a row on the sea, and he told me some things.'

'What sort of things?'

'Why, about us, Billy. I suppose you're the same as I am now, and know everything without learning it. What's Allexanassa Greek for?'

'Why, something like the Country of Changing Queens, isn't it?'

'And what does Plurimiregia mean?'

'That must mean the land of many Kings. Why?'

'Because that's what it is. They're always changing their Kings and Queens here, for a most horrid and frightening reason, Billy. They get them from a registry office a long way off so that they shouldn't know. Billy, there's a dreadful dragon, and he comes once a month to be fed. And they feed him with Kings and Queens! That's why we know everything without learning. Because there's no time to learn in. And the dragon has two heads, Billy— a pig's head and a lizard's head—and the pig's head is to eat *you* with and the lizard's head will eat *me*!'

'So they brought us here for that,' said Billy—'mean, cruel, cowardly brutes!'

'Mother always said you could never tell what a situation was like until you tried it,' said Eliza. 'But what are we to do? The dragon comes tomorrow. When I heard that I asked where your kingdom was, and the boatman showed me, and I made him land me here. So Allexanassa hasn't got a Queen now, but Plurimiregia has got us both.'

Billy rumpled his hair with his hands.

'Oh, my cats alive!' he said, 'we must do something; but I'll tell you what it is, Eliza. You're no end of a brick to come and tell me. You might have got off all by yourself, and left me to the pig's head.'

'No, I mightn't,' said Eliza sharply. 'I know everything that people can learn, the same as you, and that includes right and wrong. So you see I *mightn't*.'

'That's true! I wonder whether our being clever would help us? Let's take a boat and steer straight out, and take our chance. I can sail and steer beautifully.'

'So can I,' said Eliza disdainfully; 'but, you see, it's too late for that. Twenty-four hours before the beast comes the sea-water runs away, and great waves of thick treacle come sweeping round the kingdoms. No boat can live in such a sea.'

'Well, but how does the dragon get here? Is he on the island?'

'No,' said Eliza, squeezing up handfuls of herbs in her agitation till the scent quite overpowered the scent of the honeysuckle. 'No; he comes out of the sea. But he is very hot inside, and he melts the treacle so that it gets quite thin, like when it runs out of a treacle-pudding, and so he can swim in it, and he comes along to the quay, and is fed—with *Us*.'

Billy shuddered.

'I wish we were back in Claremont Square,' said he.

'So do I, I'm sure,' said Eliza. 'Though I don't know where it is, nor yet want to know.'

'Hush!' said Billy suddenly. 'I hear a rustling. It's the Prime Minister, and I can hear he's got straws in his hair again, most likely because you're disappeared, and he thinks he will have to cook the breakfast. Meet me beside the lighthouse at four this afternoon. Hide in this summer-house and don't come out till the coast's clear.'

He ran out and took the Prime Minister's arm.

'What is the straw for now?'

'Merely a bad habit,' said the Prime Minister wearily.

Then Billy suddenly saw, and he said:

'You're a beastly mean, cowardly sneak, and you feel it; that's what the straws are about!'

'Your Majesty!' said the Prime Minister feebly.

'Yes,' said Billy firmly; 'you know you are. Now, I know all the laws of Plurimiregia, and I'm going to abdicate this morning, and the next in rank has to be King if he can't engage a fresh one. You're next in rank to me, so by the time the dragon comes you'll be the King. I'll attend your Coronation.'

The Prime Minister gasped, 'How did you find out?' and turned the colour of unripe peaches.

'That's telling,' said Billy. 'If you hadn't all been such sneaks, I expect heaps of your Kings had sense enough to have got rid of the dragon for you. Only I suppose you've never told them in time. Now, look here. I don't want you to do anything except keep you mouth shut, and let there be a boat, and no boatman, on the beach under the lighthouse at four o'clock.'

'But the sea's all treacle.'

'I said on the beach, not on the sea, my good straw merchant. And what I say you've jolly well got to do. You must be there—and no one else. If you tell a soul I'll abdicate, and where will you be then?'

'I don't know,' said the wretched Prime Minister, stooping to gather some more straws from the strawberry bed.

'But I do,' said Billy. 'Now for breakfast.'

Before four o'clock that afternoon the Prime Minister's head was a perfect bird's-nest of straws. But he met Billy at the appointed place, and there was a boat—and also Eliza. Billy carried his Lee-Metford.

A wind blew from the shore, and the straws in the Prime Minister's hair rustled like a barley-field in August.

'Now,' said Billy the King, 'my Royal Majesty commands you to speak to the dragon as soon as it arrives, and to say that your King has abdicated——'

'But he hasn't,' said the Prime Minister in tears.

'But he *does now*—so you won't be telling a lie. I abdicate. But I give you my word of honour I'll turn King again as soon as I've tried my little plan. I shall be quite in time to meet my fate—and the dragon. Say "The King has abdicated. You'd better just look in at Allexanassa and get the Queen, and when you call again I'll have a nice fat King all ready for you."'

Billy had never felt so truly regal as now, when he was preparing to risk his life in order to save his subjects from the monthly temptation to be mean and cowardly and sneakish. I think myself it was good of Billy. He might just have abdicated and let things slide. Some boys would have.

The sea of greeny-black treacle heaved and swelled sulkily against the beach. The straws trembled, and the Prime Minister said:

'Very well; I'll do it. But I'd sooner die than see my King false to his word.'

'You won't have to choose between the two,' said Billy, very pale, but determined. 'Your King's not a hound, like —like some people.'

And then, far away on the very edge of the green treacly sea, they saw a squirming and a squelching and clouds of steam, and all sorts of exciting and unpleasant things happening very suddenly and all together.

The Prime Minister covered his head with dry seaweed and said:

'That's Him.'

'That's *He*,' corrected Eliza the Queen and Billy the King in one breath.

But the Prime Minister was long past any proper pride in his grammar.

And then, cutting its way through the thick, sticky waves of the treacle sea, came the hot dragon, melting a way for himself as he came. And he got nearer and nearer and bigger and bigger, and at last he came close to the beach, snouting and snorting, and opened two great mouths in an expecting, hungry sort of way; and when he found he was not being fed the expression of the mouths changed to an angry and surprised question. And one mouth was a pig's mouth and one was a lizard's.

15

Billy the King borrowed a pin from Eliza the Queen to
stick into the Prime Minister, who was by this time nearly
buried in the seaweed which he had been trying to arrange
in his hair.

'Speak up, silly!' said His Majesty.

The Prime Minister spoke up.

'Please, sir,' he said to the two-headed dragon, 'our King
has abdicated, so we've nothing for you just now, but if
you could just run over to Allexanassa and pick up their
Queen, we'll have a nice fat King ready for you if you'll
call on your way home.'

The Prime Minister shuddered as he spoke. He happened to be very fat.

The dragon did not say a word. He nodded with both
his heads and grunted with both his mouths, and turned
his one tail and swam away along the track of thin, warm
treacle which he had made in swimming across the sea.

Quick as thought, Billy the King signed to the Prime
Minister and to Eliza, and they launched the boat. Billy
sprang on board and pushed off, and it was not till the boat
was a dozen yards from shore that he turned to wave a
farewell to Eliza and the Prime Minister. The latter was
indeed still on the beach, searching hopefully among the

drifts and weeds for more straws, to mark his sense of the constitutional crisis, but Eliza had disappeared.

Then—'I'm here,' said a thick voice.

And, sure enough, there was Eliza, holding on to the gunwale of the boat and swimming heavily in the warm treacle. Nearly choked with it, too, for she had been under more than once.

Billy hastened to haul her aboard, and, though she was quite brown and very, very sticky, the moment she was safe in the boat he threw his arms round her and said:

'Dear, darling Eliza, you're the dearest, bravest girl in the world. If we ever get out of this you'll marry me, won't you? There's no one in the world like you. Say you will.'

'Of course I will,' said Eliza, still spluttering through the treacle. 'There's no one in the world like you, either.'

'Right! Then, if that's so, you steer and I'll sail, and we'll get the better of the beast yet,' said Billy.

And he set the sail, and Eliza steered as well as she could in her treacly state.

About the middle of the channel they caught up with the dragon. Billy took up his Lee-Metford and fired its eight bullets straight into the dragon's side. You have no idea

how the fire spurted out through the bullet-holes. But the wind from shore had caught the sails, and the boat was now going very much faster than the dragon, who found the bullet-holes annoying, and had slowed up to see what was the matter.

'Good-bye, you dear, brave Eliza,' said Billy the King. '*You're* all right, anyhow.'

And, holding his reloaded Lee-Metford rifle high over his head, he plunged into the treacly sea and swam back towards the dragon. It is very difficult to shoot straight when you are swimming, especially in nearly boiling treacle, but His Majesty King Billy managed to do it. He sent his eight bullets straight into the dragon's heads, and the huge monster writhed and wriggled and squirmed and squawked, all over the sea from end to end, till at last it floated limply on the surface of the clear, warm treacle, and stretched its paws out, shut its eyes, all four of them, and died. The lizard's eyes shut last.

Then Billy began to swim for dear life towards the shore of Plurimiregia, and the treacle was so hot that if he hadn't been a King he would have been boiled. But now that the dreadful dragon was cold in death there was nothing to keep the treacle sea thin and warm, and it began to thicken so fast that swimming was very difficult indeed. If you don't understand this, you need only ask the attendants at your nearest swimming-baths to fill the baths with treacle instead of water, and you will very soon comprehend how it was that Billy reached the shore of his kingdom quite exhausted and almost speechless.

The Prime Minister was there. He had fetched a whole truss of straw when he thought Billy's plan had failed, and that the dragon would eat him as the next in rank, and he wanted to do the thing thoroughly; and when he warmly embraced the treacly King, Billy became so covered with straws that he hardly knew himself. He pulled himself together, however, enough to withdraw his resignation, and then looked out over the sea. In mid-channel lay the dead dragon, and far in the distance he could see the white sails of the boat nearing the shores of Allexanassa.

'And what are we to do now?' asked the Prime Minister.

'Have a bath,' said the King. 'The dragon's dead, and I'll fetch Eliza in the morning. They won't hurt her over there now the dragon's killed.'

'*They* won't hurt her,' said the Prime Minister. 'It's the treacle. Allexanassa is an island. The dragon brought the treacle up by his enchantments, and now there is no one to take it away again. You'll never get a boat to live in a sea like that—never.'

'Won't I?' said Billy. 'I'm cleverer than you.'

But, all the same, he didn't quite see his way to sailing a boat in that sea, and with a sad and aching heart he went back to the palace to the silver bath. The treacle and straws took hours to wash off, and after that he was so tired that he did not want any supper, which was just as well, be-

cause there was no one to cook it. Tired as he was, Billy slept very badly. He woke up again and again to wonder what had become of his brave little friend, and to wish that he could have done something to prevent her being carried away in that boat; but, think as he might, he failed to see that he could have done any differently. And his heart sank, for, in spite of his bold words to the Prime Minister, he had no more idea than you have how to cross the sea of thick treacle that lay between his kingdom and Allexanassa. He invented steamships with red-hot screws and paddle-wheels all through his dreams, and when he got up in the morning he looked out of his window on the dark sea and longed for a good, gray, foamy, salt, tumbling sea like we have at home in England, no matter how high the waves and the winds might be. But the wind had fallen, and the dark brown sea looked strangely calm.

Hastily snatching a dozen peaches out of the palace garden by way of breakfast, Billy the King hurried to the beach by the lighthouse. No heaving of the treacle sea broke the smooth line of it against the beach. Billy looked —looked again, swallowed the last peach, stone and all, and tore back to the town.

He rushed into the chief ironmonger's and bought a pair of skates and a gimlet. In less time than I can write it he had scurried back to the beach, bored holes in his gold heels, fastened on the skates, and was skating away over the brown sea towards Allexanassa. For the treacle, heated to boiling-point by the passing of the dragon, had now grown cold, and, of course, it was now *toffee*! Far off, Eliza had had the same idea as soon as she saw the toffee, and, of course, as Queen of Allexanassa, she could skate beauti-fully. So the two skated into each other's arms somewhere

near the middle of the channel between the two islands.

They stood telling each other how happy they were for a few moments, or it may have been a few hours; and when they turned to go back to Plurimiregia they found that the toffee-ice of the treacle sea was black with crowds of skaters—for the Allexanassians and the Plurimiregians had found out the wonderful truth, and were hurrying across to pay visits to their friends and relations in the opposite islands. Near the shore the toffee was hidden by troops of children, who had borrowed the family hammers and were chipping into the solid toffee and eating the flakes of it as they splintered off.

People were pointing out to each other the spot where the dragon had sunk, and when they perceived Billy the King and Eliza the Queen they sent up a shout that you could have heard miles out at sea—if there had been any sea—which, of course, there wasn't. The Prime Minister had lost no time in issuing a proclamation setting forth Billy's splendid conduct in ridding the country of the dragon, and all the populace were in a frenzy of gratitude and loyalty.

Billy turned on a little tap inside his head by some means which I cannot describe to you, and a bright flood of cleverness poured through his brain.

'After all,' he said to Eliza, 'they were going to give us to the dragon to save their own lives. It's bad, I know. But I dont't know that it's worse than people who let other people die of lead-poisoning because they want a particular glaze on their dinner-plates, or let people die of phosphor-us-poisoning so that they may get matches at six boxes a penny. We're as well off here as in England.'

'Yes,' said Eliza.

So they agreed to stay and go on being King and Queen, on condition that the Prime Minister consented to give up straws altogether, even in moments of crisis.

Eliza and Billy were married in due course. The king-doms are now extremely happy.

So that's all right.

Exploring expeditions were fitted out to find the edge of the toffee. It was found to stand up in cliffs two hundred feet high, overhanging the real, live, salt-watery sea. The King had ships built at once to sail on the real sea and carry merchandise to other lands. And so Allexanassa and Plurimiregia grew richer and richer every day. The mer-chandise, of course, is toffee, and half the men in the king-doms work in the great toffee-mines. All the toffee you buy in shops comes from there. And the reason why some of the cheaper kinds you buy are so gritty, I need hardly say, is because the toffee-miners will not remember, before they go down into the mines, to wipe their muddy boots on the doormats provided by Billy the King, with the Royal Arms in seven colours on the middle of each mat.

The Charmed Life
or the
Princess and the Lift-man

The Charmed Life

This may well be the earliest fairy-tale in print in which a modern lift is given a prominent part. Lifts were a real novelty when E. Nesbit was writing; as you may have noticed, she loved to bring modern machines and gadgets into her magic. The idea of the 'charmed life', on the other hand, is as old as the oldest legends. You will find it, in one form or another, in most collections of real fairy tales. In one version, for instance, a giant hides his heart in a secret place. When it is found, he is lost.

How strange to think that, when E.N. was writing this, at the beginning of the century, every European country had a reigning monarch; that everywhere real emperors, kings and princes had real courts. The notion of a working prince—an engineer, what's more—was quite a daring one. Of course, there was Andersen's swineherd-prince, but he was merely using a disguise. The reference to Sherlock Holmes is interesting, for that great detective had only recently turned up on the scene. The first of the Holmes books (*The Adventures of Sherlock Holmes*) was published in 1891; separate stories continued to appear in the *Strand Magazine* for a number of years, before being published in book form. E. Nesbit's fairy tales (most of which were also first published in the *Strand Magazine* during the same period as Conan Doyle's) followed a similar path.

N.L.

THERE WAS ONCE a Prince whose father failed in business and lost everything he had in the world—crown, kingdom, money, jewels, and friends. This was because he was so fond of machinery that he was always making working models of things he invented, and so had no time to attend to the duties that Kings are engaged for. So he lost his situation. There is a King in French history who was fond of machinery, particularly clock-work, and he lost everything too, even his head. The King in this story kept his head, however, and when he wasn't allowed to make laws any more, he was quite contented to go on making machines. And as his machines were a great deal better than his laws had ever been, he soon got a nice little business together, and was able to buy a house in another kingdom, and settle down comfortably with his wife and son. The house was one of those delightful villas called after Queen Anne (the one whose death is still so often mentioned and so justly deplored), with stained glass to the front-door, and coloured tiles on the front-garden path, and gables where there was never need of gables, and nice geraniums and calceolarias in the front-garden, and pretty red brick on the front of the house. The back of the house was yellow brick, because that did not show so much.

Here the King and the Queen and the Prince lived very pleasantly. The Queen snipped the dead geraniums off with a pair of gold scissors, and did fancy-work for bazaars. The Prince went to the Red-Coat School, and the King worked up his business. In due time the Prince was apprenticed to his father's trade: and a very industrious apprentice he was, and never had anything to do with the idle apprentices who play pitch and toss on tombstones, as you see in Mr Hogarth's picture.

When the Prince was twenty-one his mother called him to her. She put down the blotting-book she was embroidering for the School Bazaar in a tasteful pattern of stocks and nasturtiums, and said:

'My dear son, you have had the usual coming-of-age presents—silver cigar-case and match-box; a handsome set of brushes with your initials on the back; a Gladstone bag, also richly initialled; the complete works of Dickens and Thackeray; a Swan fountain-pen mounted in gold; and the heartfelt blessing of your father and mother. But there is still one more present for you.'

'You are too good, mamma,' said the Prince, fingering the nasturtium-coloured silks.

'Don't fidget,' said the Queen, 'and listen to me. When you were a baby a fairy, who was your godmother, gave you a most valuable present—a Charmed Life. As long as you keep it safely, nothing can harm you.'

'How delightful!' said the Prince. 'Why, mamma, you might have let me go to sea when I wanted to. It would have been quite safe.'

'Yes, my dear,' said the Queen, 'but it's best to be careful. I have taken care of your life all these years, but now you are old enough to take care of it for yourself. Let me advise you to keep it in a safe place. You should never carry valuables about on your person.'

And then she handed the Charmed Life over to him, and he took it and kissed her, and thanked her and then went away and hid it. He took a brick out of the wall of the villa, and hid his Life behind it. The bricks in the walls of these Queen Anne villas generally come out quite easily.

Now, the father of the Prince had been King of Bohemia, so, of course, the Prince was called Florizel, which is their family name; but when the King went into business he went in as Rex Bloomsbury, and his great patent Lightning Lift Company called itself R. Bloomsbury and Co., so that the Prince was known as F. Bloomsbury, which was as near as the King dared go to 'Florizel, Prince of Bohemia.' His mother, I am sorry to say, called him Florrie till he was quite grown up.

Now, the King of the country where Florizel lived was a very go-ahead sort of man, and as soon as he heard that there were such things as lifts—which was not for a long time, because no one ever lets a King know anything if it can be helped—he ordered one of the very, very best for his palace. Next day a card was brought in by one of the palace footmen. It had on it: 'Mr. F. Bloomsbury, R. Bloomsbury and Co.'

'Show him in,' said the King.

'Good-morning, sire,' said Florizel, bowing with that perfect grace which is proper to Princes.

'Good-morning, young man,' said the King. 'About this lift, now.'

'Yes, sire. May I ask how much your Majesty is pre-

27

pared to——'

'Oh, never mind price,' said the King; 'it all comes out of the taxes.'

'I should think, then, that Class A . . . our special Argentinella design—white satin cushions, woodwork overlaid with ivory and inset with pearls, opals, and silver.'

'Gold,' said the King shortly.

'Not with pearls and ivory,' said Florizel firmly. He had excellent taste. 'The gold pattern—we call it the Anriradia —is inlaid with sapphires, emeralds, and black diamonds.'

'I'll have the gold pattern,' said the King; 'but you might run up a little special lift for the Princess's apartments. I dare say she'd like that Argentinella pattern— "Simple and girlish," I see it says in your circular.'

So Florizel booked the order, and the gold and sapphire and emerald lift was made and fixed, and all the Court was so delighted that it spent its whole time in going up and down in it, and there had to be new blue satin cushions within a week.

Then the Prince superintended the fixing of the Princess's lift—the Argentinella design—and the Princess Candida herself came to look on at the works; and she and Florizel met, and their eyes met, and their hands met, because his caught hers, and dragged her back, just in time to save her from being crushed by a heavy steel bar that was being lowered into its place.

'Why, you've saved my life,' said the Princess.

But Florizel could say nothing. His heart was beating too fast, and it seemed to be beating in his throat, and not in its proper place behind his waistcoat.

'Who are you?' said the Princess.

'I'm an engineer,' said the Prince.

'Oh dear!' said the Princess, 'I thought you were a Prince. I'm sure you look more like a Prince than any Prince *I've* ever seen.'

'I wish I was a Prince,' said Florizel; 'but I never wished it till three minutes ago.'

The Princess smiled, and then she frowned, and then she went away.

Florizel went straight back to the office, where his father, Mr Rex Bloomsbury, was busy at his knee-hole writing-table.

He spent the morning at the office, and the afternoon in the workshop.

'Father,' he said, 'I don't know what ever will become of me. I wish I was a Prince!'

The King and Queen of Bohemia had never let their son know that he was a Prince; for what is the use of being a Prince if there's never going to be a kingdom for you?

Now, the King, who was called R. Bloomsbury, Esq., looked at his son over his spectacles and said:

'Why?'

'Because I've been and gone and fallen head over ears in love with the Princess Candida.'

The father rubbed his nose thoughtfully with his fountain pen.

'Humph!' he said; 'you've fixed your choice high.'

'Choice!' cried the Prince distractedly. 'There wasn't much choice about it. She just looked at me, and there I was, don't you know? I didn't *want* to fall in love like this. Oh, father, it hurts most awfully! What ever shall I do?'

After a long pause, full of thought, his father replied:

'Bear it, I suppose.'

'But I *can't* bear it—at least, not unless I can see her every day. Nothing else in the world matters in the least.'

'Dear me!' said his father.

'Couldn't I disguise myself as a Prince, and try to make her like me a little?'

'The disguise you suggest is quite beyond our means at present.'

'Then I'll disguise myself as a lift attendant,' said Florizel.

And what is more, he did it. His father did not interfere. He believed in letting young people manage their own love affairs.

So then when the lift was finished, and the Princess and her ladies crowded round to make the first ascent in it, there was Florizel dressed in white satin knee-breeches, and coat with mother-o'-pearl buttons. He had silver buckles to his shoes, and a tiny opal breast-pin on the lappet of his coat, where the white flower goes at weddings.

When the Princess saw him she said:

'Now, none of you girls are to go in the lift at all, mind! It's *my* lift. You can use the other one, or go up the mother-of-pearl staircase, as usual.'

Then she stepped into the lift, and the silver doors clicked, and the lift went up, just carrying her and him.

She had put on a white silky gown, to match the new

lift, and she, too, had silver buckles on her shoes, and a string of pearls round her throat, and a silver chain set with opals in her dark hair; and she had a bunch of jasmine flowers at her neck. As the lift went out of sight the youngest lady-in-waiting whispered:

'What a pretty pair! Why, they're made for each other! What a pity he's a lift-man! He looks exactly like a Prince.'

'Hold your tongue, silly!' said the eldest lady-in-waiting, and slapped her.

The Princess went up and down in the lift all the morning, and when at last she had to step out of it because the palace luncheon-bell had rung three times, and the roast peacock was getting cold, the eldest lady-in-waiting noticed that the Lift-man had a jasmine flower fastened to his coat with a little opal pin.

The eldest lady-in-waiting kept a sharp eye on the Princess, but after the first day the Princess only seemed to go up and down in the lift when it was really necessary, and then she always took the youngest lady-in-waiting with her; so that though the Lift-man always had a flower in his buttonhole, there was no reason to suppose it had not been given him by his mother.

'I suppose I'm a silly, suspicious little thing,' said the eldest lady-in-waiting. 'Of course, it was the lift that amused her, just at first. How *could* a Princess be interested in a lift-man ?'

Now, when people are in love, and want to be quite certain that they are loved in return, they will take any risks to find out what they want to know. But as soon as they are *quite sure*, they begin to be careful.

And after those seventy-five ups and downs in the lift, on the first day, the Princess no longer had any doubt that she was beloved by the Lift-man. Not that he had said a word about it, but she was a clever Princess, and she had seen how he picked up the jasmine flower she let fall, and kissed it when she pretended she wasn't looking and he pretended he didn't know she was. Of course, she had been in love with him ever since they met, and their eyes met, and their hands. She told herself it was because he had saved her life, but that wasn't the real reason at all.

So, being quite sure, she began to be careful.

'Since he really loves me he'll find a way to tell me so, right out. It's his part, not mine, to make everything pos-

sible,' she said.

As for Florizel, he was quite happy. He saw her every day, and every day when he took his place in his lift there was a fresh jasmine flower lying on the satin cushion. And he pinned it into his buttonhole and wore it there all day, and thought of his lady, and of how that first wonderful day she had dropped a jasmine flower, and how he had picked it up when she pretended she was not looking, and he was pretending that he did not know she was. But all the same he wanted to know exactly how that jasmine flower came there every day, and whose hand brought it. It might be the youngest lady-in-waiting, but Florizel didn't think so.

So he went to the palace one morning bright and early, much earlier than usual, and there was no jasmine flower. Then he hid behind one of the white velvet window-curtains of the corridor and waited. And, presently, who should come stealing along on the tips of her pink toes—so as to make no noise at all—but the Princess herself, fresh as the morning in a white muslin frock with a silver ribbon

33

round her waist, and a bunch of jasmine at her neck. She took one of the jasmine flowers and kissed it and laid it on the white satin seat of the lift, and when she stepped back there was the Lift-man.

'Oh!' said Candida, and blushed like a child that is caught in mischief.

'Oh!' said Florizel, and he picked up the jasmine and kissed it many times.

'Why do you do that?' said the Princess.

'Because you did,' said the Prince. 'I saw you. Do you want to go on pretending any more?'

The Princess did not know what to say, so she said nothing.

Florizel came and stood quite close to her.

'I used to wish I was a Prince,' he said, 'but I don't now. I'd rather be an engineer. If I'd been a Prince I should never have seen you.'

'I don't want you to be a bit different,' said the Princess. And she stopped to smell the jasmine in his buttonhole.

'So we're betrothed,' said Florizel.

'Are we?' said Candida.

'Aren't we?' he said.

'Well, yes, I suppose we are,' said she.

'Very well, then,' said Florizel, and he kissed the Princess.

'You're sure you don't mind marrying an engineer?' he said, when she had kissed him back.

'Of course not,' said the Princess.

'Then I'll buy the ring,' said he, and kissed her again.

Then she gave him the rest of the jasmine, with a kiss for each star, and he gave her a keepsake in return, and they parted.

34

'My heart is yours,' said Florizel, 'and my life is in your hands.'

'My life is yours,' said she, 'and my heart is in your heart.'

Now, I am sorry to say that somebody had been listening all the time behind another curtain, and when the Princess had gone to breakfast and the Lift-man had gone down in his lift, this somebody came out and said, 'Aha!'

It was a wicked, disagreeable, snub-nosed page-boy, who would have liked to marry the Princess himself. He had really no chance, and never could have had, because his father was only a rich brewer. But he felt himself to be much superior to a lift-man. And he was the kind of boy who always sneaks if he has half a chance. So he went and told the King that he had seen the Princess kissing the Lift-man in the morning all bright and early.

The King said he was a lying hound, and put him in prison at once for mentioning such a thing—which served him right.

Then the King thought it best to find out for himself whether the snub-nosed page-boy had spoken the truth.

So he watched in the morning all bright and early, and he saw the Princess come stealing along on the tips of her little pink toes, and the lift (Argentinella design) came up, and the Lift-man in it. And the Princess gave him kissed

jasmine to put in his buttonhole.

So the King jumped out on them and startled them dreadfully. And Florizel was locked up in prison, and the Princess was locked up in her room with only the eldest lady-in-waiting to keep her company. And the Princess cried all day and all night. And she managed to hide the keepsake the Prince had given her. She hid it in a little book of verses. And the eldest lady saw her do it. Florizel was condemned to be executed for having wanted to marry someone so much above him in station. But when the axe fell on his neck the axe flew to pieces, and the neck was not hurt at all. So they sent for another axe and tried again. And again the axe splintered and flew. And when they picked up the bits of the axe they had all turned to leaves of poetry books.

So they put off the execution till next day.

The gaoler told the snub-nosed page all about it when he took him his dinner of green water and mouldering crusts.

'Couldn't do the trick!' said the gaoler. 'Two axes broke off short and the bits turned to rubbish. The executioner says the rascal has a Charmed Life.'

'Of course he has,' said the page, sniffing at the crusts with his snub-nose. 'I know all about that, but I shan't tell unless the King gives me a free pardon and something fit to eat. Roast pork and onion stuffing, I think. And you can tell him so.'

So the gaoler told the King. And the King gave the snub-nosed page the pardon and the pork, and then the page said:

'He has a Charmed Life. I heard him tell the Princess so. And what is more, he gave it to her to keep. And she said she'd hide it in a safe place!'

Then the King told the eldest lady-in-waiting to watch, and she did watch, and saw the Princess take Florizel's Charmed Life and hide it in a bunch of jasmine. So she took the jasmine and gave it to the King, and he burnt it. But the Princess had not left the Life in the jasmine.

Then they tried to hang Florizel, because, of course, he had an ordinary life as well as a charmed one, and the King wished him to be without any life at all.

Thousands of people crowded to see the presumptuous Lift-man hanged, and the execution lasted the whole morning, and seven brand new ropes were wasted one after the other, and they all left off being ropes and turned into long wreaths of jasmine, which broke into bits rather than hang such a handsome Lift-man.

The King was furious. But he was not too furious to see that the Princess must have taken the Charmed Life out from the jasmine flowers, and put it somewhere else, when the eldest lady-in-waiting was not looking.

And it turned out afterwards that the Princess had held Florizel's life in her hand all the time the execution was going on. The eldest lady-in-waiting was clever, but she was not so clever as the Princess.

The next morning the eldest lady brought the Princess's silver mirror to the King.

'The Charmed Life is in that, your Majesty,' she said. 'I saw the Princess put it in.'

And so she had, but she had not seen the Princess take it out again almost directly afterwards.

The King smashed the looking-glass, and gave orders that poor Florizel was to be drowned in the palace fishpond.

So they tied big stones to his hands and feet and threw him in. And the stones changed to corks and held him up, and he swam to land, and when they arrested him as he landed they found that on each of the corks there was a beautiful painting of Candida's face, as she saw it every morning in her mirror.

Now, the King and Queen of Bohemia, Florizel's father and mother, had gone to Margate for a fortnight's holiday. 'We will have a thorough holiday,' said the King; 'we will forget the world, and not even look at a newspaper.'

But on the third day they both got tired of forgetting the world, and each of them secretly bought a newspaper and read it on the beach, and each rushed back and met the other on the steps of the boarding-house where they were staying. And the Queen began to cry, and the King took her in his arms on the doorstep, to the horror of the other boarders, who were looking out of the windows at them; and then they rushed off to the railway station, leaving behind them their luggage and the astonished boarders, and took a special train to town. Because the King had read in his newspaper, and the Queen in hers, that the Lift-man was being executed every morning from nine to twelve; and though, so far, none of the executions had ended fatally, yet at any moment the Prince's Charmed Life might be taken, and then there would be an end of the daily executions—a very terrible end.

Arrived at the capital, the poor Queen of Bohemia got into a hansom with the King, and they were driven to the palace. The palace-yard was crowded.

'What is the matter?' the King of Bohemia asked.

'It's that Lift-man,' said a bystander, with spectacles and a straw hat; 'he has as many lives as a cat. They tried boiling oil this morning, and the oil turned into white-rose leaves, and the fire under it turned to a white-rose bush. And now the King has sent for Princess Candida, and is going to have it out with her. The whole thing has been most exciting.'

'I should think so,' said the Lift-man's father.

He gave his arm to his wife, and they managed to squeeze through to the great council hall, where the King of that country sat on his gold throne, surrounded by lords-in-waiting, judges in wigs, and other people in other things.

Florizel was there loaded with chains, and standing in a very noble attitude at one corner of the throne steps. At the other stood the Princess, looking across at her lover.

'Now,' said the King, 'I am tired of diplomacy and tact, and the eldest lady-in-waiting is less of a Sherlock Holmes than I thought her, so let us be straightforward and honest. Have you got a Charmed Life?'

'I haven't exactly got it,' said Florizel. 'My life is not my own now.'

'Did he give it to you?' the King asked his daughter.

'I cannot tell a lie, father,' said the Princess, just as

though her name had been George Washington instead of Candida; 'he did give it to me.'

'What have you done with it?'

'I have hidden it in different places. I have saved it; he saved mine once.'

'Where is it?' asked her father, 'as you so justly observe you cannot tell a lie.'

'If I tell you,' said the Princess, 'will you give your Royal word that the execution you have ordered for this morning shall be really the last? You can destroy the object that I have hidden his Charmed Life in, and then you can destroy him. But you must promise me not to ask me to hide his Life in any new place, because I am tired of hide-and-seek.'

All the judges and lords-in-waiting and people felt really sorry for the Princess, for they thought that all these executions had turned her brain.

'I give you my Royal word,' said the King upon his throne. 'I won't ask you to hide his Life any more. Indeed, I was against the practice from the first. Now, where have you hidden his Life?'

'In my heart,' said the Princess, brave and clear, so that everyone heard her in the big hall. 'You can't take his Life without taking mine, and if you take mine you may as well take his, for he won't care to go on living without me.'

She sprang across the throne steps to Florizel, and his fetters jangled as she threw her arms round him.

'Dear me!' said the King, rubbing his nose with his sceptre; 'this is very awkward.'

But the father and mother of Florizel had wriggled and wormed their way through the crowd to a front place, and now the father spoke.

'Your Majesty, allow me. Perhaps I can assist your decision.'

'Oh, all right,' said the King upon his throne; 'go ahead. I'm struck all of a heap.'

'You see before you,' said the King of Bohemia, 'one known to the world of science and of business as R. Bloomsbury, inventor and patenter of many mechanical novelties —among others the Patent Lightning Lift—now formed into a company of which I am chairman. The young Liftman—whose fetters are most clumsily designed, if you will pardon my saying so—is my son.'

'Of course he's somebody's son,' said the King upon his throne.

'Well, he happens to be mine, and I gather that you do not think him a good enough match for your daughter.'

'Without wishing to hurt your feelings——' began Candida's father.

'Exactly. Well, know, O King on your throne, and everyone else, that this young Lift-Man is no other than Florizel,

Prince of Bohemia. I am the King of Bohemia, and this is my Queen.'

As he spoke he took his crown out of his pocket and put it on. His wife took off her bonnet and got her crown out of her reticule and put that on, and Florizel's crown was handed to the Princess, who fitted it on for him, because his hands were awkward with chains.

'Your most convincing explanation alters everything,' said the King upon his throne, and he came down to meet the visitors. 'Bless you, my children! Strike off his chains, can't you? I hope there's no ill-feeling, Florizel,' he added, turning to the Prince. 'Will half an hour from now suit you for the wedding?'

So they were married, and they still live very happily. They will live as long as is good for them, and when Candida dies Florizel will die too, because she still carries his Life in her heart.

Melisande
or Long and Short Division

Melisande

One of the liveliest and wittiest of the Nesbit magic shorter tales, this is also one of several unexpectedly bringing in tricks with numbers—a teasing kind of fairy tale arithmetic, or even geometry. (*Fortunatus Rex* is another.) If you are reminded now and then of *Rapunzel, Alice, Gulliver* or *The Rose and the Ring* (can you track down where?), remember that all fairy tales grow out of other fairy tales, (the same holds for people, flowers, cats—almost everything grows from its ancestors), and yet the result is always something new. (A poem that you may know by Walter de la Mare, 'Very Old are the Woods', sets this out perfectly.) In fact, quite a few points which sound like genuine ancient magic lore turn out to be genuine Nesbit inventions: for instance—'A fairy who breaks the traditions of fairy history goes out . . . like the flame of a candle. And all traditions show that only *one* bad fairy is ever forgotten at a christening party'. One of the best of all the Nesbit fairies may be found in *Melisande*. True, she never actually appears, but this hardly matters. She is the one who dashes off those cheerful little notes about the wish. Look out for her.

N.L.

WHEN THE PRINCESS MELISANDE was born, her mother, the Queen, wished to have a christening party, but the King put his foot down and said he would not have it.

'I've seen too much trouble come of christening parties,' said he. 'However carefully you keep your visiting-book, some fairy or other is sure to get left out, and you know what *that* leads to. Why, even in my own family, the most shocking things have occurred. The Fairy Malevola was not asked to my great-grandmother's christening—and you know all about the spindle and the hundred years' sleep.'

'Perhaps you're right,' said the Queen. 'My own cousin by marriage forgot some stuffy old fairy or other when she was sending out the cards for her daughter's christening, and the old wretch turned up at the last moment, and the girl drops toads out of her mouth to this day.'

'Just so. And then there was that business of the mouse and the kitchen-maids,' said the King; 'we'll have no non-sense about it. I'll be her godfather, and you shall be her godmother, and we won't ask a single fairy; then none of them can be offended.'

'Unless they all are,' said the Queen.

And that was exactly what happened. When the King and the Queen and the baby got back from the christening the parlourmaid met them at the door, and said—

'Please, your Majesty, several ladies have called. I told them you were not at home, but they all said they'd wait.'

'Are they in the parlour ?' asked the Queen.

'I've shown them into the Throne Room, your Majesty,' said the parlourmaid. 'You see, there are several of them.'

There were about seven hundred. The great Throne Room was crammed with fairies, of all ages and of all degrees of beauty and ugliness—good fairies and bad fairies, flower fairies and moon fairies, fairies like spiders and fairies like butterflies—and as the Queen opened the door and began to say how sorry she was to have kept them waiting, they all cried, with one voice, 'Why didn't you ask *me* to your christening party ?'

'I haven't had a party,' said the Queen, and she turned to the King and whispered, 'I told you so.' This was her only consolation.

'You've had a christening,' said the fairies, all together.

'I'm very sorry,' said the poor Queen, but Malevola pushed forward and said, 'Hold your tongue,' most rudely.

Malevola is the oldest, as well as the most wicked, of the fairies. She is deservedly unpopular, and has been left out of more christening parties than all the rest of the fairies put together.

'Don't begin to make excuses,' she said, shaking her finger at the Queen. 'That only makes your conduct worse. You know well enough what happens if a fairy is left out of a christening party. We are all going to give our christening presents *now*. As the fairy of highest social position, I shall begin. The Princess shall be bald.'

The Queen nearly fainted, as Malevola drew back, and another fairy, in a smart bonnet with snakes in it, stepped forward with a rustle of bats' wings. But the King stepped forward too.

'No you don't!' said he. 'I wonder at you, ladies, I do indeed. How can you be so unfairylike ? Have none of you been to school—have none of you studied the history of your own race ? Surely you don't need a poor, ignorant King like me to tell you that this is *no go* ?'

'How dare you ?' cried the fairy in the bonnet, and the snakes in it quivered as she tossed her head. 'It is my turn, and I say that the Princess shall be——'

The King actually put his hand over her mouth.

'Look here,' he said; 'I won't have it. Listen to reason— or you'll be sorry afterwards. A fairy who breaks the traditions of fairy history goes out—you know she does—like the flame of a candle. And all tradition shows that only *one* bad fairy is ever forgotten at a christening party and the good ones are always invited; so either this is not a christening party, or else you were all invited except one, and, by her own showing, that was Malevola. It nearly always is. Do I make myself clear ?'

Several of the better-class fairies who had been led away by Malevola's influence murmured that there was something in what His Majesty said.

'Try it, if you don't believe me,' said the King; 'give your nasty gifts to my innocent child—but as sure as you do, out you go, like a candle-flame. Now, then, will you risk it ?'

No one answered, and presently several fairies came up to the Queen and said what a pleasant party it had been, but they really must be going. This example decided the rest. One by one all the fairies said goodbye and thanked the Queen for the delightful afternoon they had spent with her.

'It's been quite too lovely,' said the lady with the snake-bonnet; '*do* ask us again soon, dear Queen. I shall be so *longing* to see you again, and the *dear* baby,' and off she went, with the snake-trimming quivering more than ever.

When the very last fairy was gone the Queen ran to look at the baby—she tore off its Honiton lace cap and burst into tears. For all the baby's downy golden hair came off with the cap, and the Princess Melisande was as bald as an egg.

'Don't cry, my love,' said the King. 'I have a wish lying by, which I've never had occasion to use. My fairy god-mother gave it me for a wedding present, but since then I've had nothing to wish for!'

'Thank you, dear,' said the Queen, smiling through her tears.

'I'll keep the wish till baby grows up,' the King went on. 'And then I'll give it to her, and if she likes to wish for hair she can.'

'Oh, won't you wish for it *now*?' said the Queen, dropping mixed tears and kisses on the baby's round, smooth head.

'No, dearest. She may want something else more when she grows up. And besides, her hair may grow by itself.'

But it never did. Princess Melisande grew up as beautiful as the sun and as good as gold, but never a hair grew on that little head of hers. The Queen sewed her little caps of green silk, and the Princess's pink and white face looked out of these like a flower peeping out of its bud. And every day as she grew older she grew dearer, and as she grew dearer she grew better, and as she grew more good she grew more beautiful.

Now, when she was grown up the Queen said to the King—

'My love, our dear daughter is old enough to know what she wants. Let her have the wish.'

So the King wrote to his fairy godmother and sent the letter by a butterfly. He asked if he might hand on to his daughter the wish the fairy had given for a wedding present.

'I have never had occasion to use it,' said he, 'though it has always made me happy to remember that I had such a thing in the house. The wish is as good as new, and my daughter is now of an age to appreciate so valuable a present.'

To which the fairy replied by return of butterfly:—

DEAR KING,—Pray do whatever you like with my poor little present. I had quite forgotten it, but I am pleased to think that you have treasured my humble keepsake all these years.

Your affectionate godmother,
FORTUNA F.

So the King unlocked his gold safe with the seven diamond-handle keys that hung at his girdle, and took out the wish and gave it to his daughter.

And Melisande said: 'Father, I will wish that all your subjects should be quite happy.'

But they were that already, because the King and Queen were so good. So the wish did not go off.

So then she said: 'Then I wish them all to be good.'

But they were that already, because they were happy. So again the wish hung fire.

Then the Queen said: 'Dearest, for my sake, wish what I tell you.'

'Why, of course I will,' said Melisande. The Queen whispered in her ear, and Melisande nodded. Then she said, aloud—

'I wish I had golden hair a yard long, and that it would grow an inch every day, and grow twice as fast every time it was cut, and——'

'Stop,' cried the King. And the wish went off, and the next moment the Princess stood smiling at him through a shower of golden hair.

'Oh, how lovely,' said the Queen. 'What a pity you interrupted her, dear; she hadn't finished.'

'What was the end?' saked the King.

'Oh,' said Melisande, 'I was only going to say, "and twice as thick."'

'It's a very good thing you didn't,' said the King. 'You've done about enough.' For he had a mathematical mind, and could do the sums about the grains of wheat on the chess-board and the nails in the horse's shoes, in his Royal head without any trouble at all.

'Why, what's the matter?' asked the Queen.

'You'll know soon enough,' said the King. 'Come, let's be happy while we may. Give me a kiss, little Melisande, and then go to nurse and ask her to teach you how to comb your hair.'

'I know,' said Melisande, 'I've often combed mother's.'

'Your mother has beautiful hair,' said the King; 'but I fancy you will find your own less easy to manage.'

And, indeed, it was so. The Princess's hair began by being a yard long, and it grew an inch every night. If you know anything at all about the simplest sums you will see that in about five weeks her hair was about two yards long. This is a very inconvenient length. It trails on the floor and sweeps up all the dust, and though in palaces, of course, it is all gold-dust, still it is not nice to have it in your hair. And the Princess's hair was growing an inch every night. When it was three yards long the Princess could not bear it any longer—it was so heavy and so hot—so she borrowed nurse's cutting-out scissors and cut it all off, and then for a few hours she was comfortable. But the hair went on growing, and now it grew twice as fast as before; so that in thirty-six days it was as long as ever. The poor Princess cried with tiredness; when she couldn't bear it any more she cut her hair and was comfortable for a very little time. For the hair now grew four times as fast as at first, and in eighteen days it was as long as before, and she had to have it cut. Then it grew eight inches a day, and the next time it was cut it grew sixteen inches a day, and then thirty-two inches and sixty-four inches and a hundred and twenty-eight inches a day, and so on, growing twice as fast after each cutting, till the Princess would go to bed at night with her hair clipped short, and wake up in the morning with yards and yards and yards of golden hair

flowing all about the room, so that she could not move
without pulling her own hair, and nurse had to come and
cut the hair off before she could get out of bed.

'I wish I was bald again,' sighed poor Melisande, looking at the little green caps she used to wear, and she cried
herself to sleep o' nights between the golden billows of the
golden hair. But she never let her mother see her cry, because it was the Queen's fault, and Melisande did not want
to seem to reproach her.

When first the Princess's hair grew her mother sent
locks of it to all her Royal relations, who had them set in
rings and brooches. Later, the Queen was able to send
enough for bracelets and girdles. But presently so much
hair was cut off that they had to burn it. Then when autumn
came all the crops failed; it seemed as though all the gold
of harvest had gone into the Princess's hair. And there was
a famine. Then Melisande said—

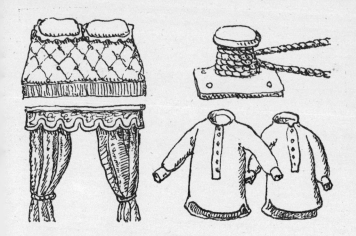

'It seems a pity to waste all my hair; it does grow so very fast. Couldn't we stuff things with it, or something, and sell them, to feed the people?'

So the King called a council of merchants, and they sent out samples of the Princess's hair, and soon orders came pouring it; and the Princess's hair became the staple export of that country. They stuffed pillows with it, and they stuffed beds with it. They made ropes of it for sailors to use, and curtains for hanging in Kings' palaces. They made haircloth of it, for hermits, and other people who wished to be uncomfy. But it was so soft and silky that it only made them happy and warm, which they did not wish to be. So the hermits gave up wearing it, and, instead, mothers bought it for their little babies, and all well-born infants wore little shirts of Princess-haircloth.

And still the hair grew and grew. And the people were fed and the famine came to an end.

Then the King said: 'It was all very well while the

famine lasted—but now I shall write to my fairy god-mother and see if something cannot be done.'

So he wrote and sent the letter by a skylark, and by return of bird came this answer—

'Why not advertise for a competent Prince? Offer the usual reward.'

So the King sent out his heralds all over the world to proclaim that any respectable Prince with proper refer-ences should marry the Princess Melisande if he could stop her hair growing.

Then from far and near came trains of Princes anxious to try their luck, and they brought all sorts of nasty things with them in bottles and round wooden boxes. The Prin-cess tried all the remedies, but she did not like any of them, and she did not like any of the Princes, so in her heart she was rather glad that none of the nasty things in bottles and boxes made the least difference to her hair.

The Princess had to sleep in the great Throne Room now, because no other room was big enough to hold her and her hair. When she woke in the morning the long high room would be quite full of her golden hair, packed tight and thick like wool in a barn. And every night when she had had the hair cut close to her head she would sit in her green silk gown by the window and cry, and kiss the little green caps she used to wear, and wish herself bald again.

It was as she sat crying there on Midsummer Eve that she first saw Prince Florizel.

He had come to the palace that evening, but he would not appear in her presence with the dust of travel on him, and she had retired with her hair borne by twenty pages before he had bathed and changed his garments and entered the reception-room.

Now he was walking in the garden in the moonlight, and
he looked up and she looked down, and for the first time
Melisande, looking on a Prince, wished that he might have
the power to stop her hair from growing. As for the Prince,
he wished many things, and the first was granted him. For
he said—

'You are Melisande?'

'And you are Florizel?'

'There are many roses round your window,' said he to
her, 'and none down here.'

She threw him one of three white roses she held in her
hand. Then he said—

'White rose trees are strong. May I climb up to you?'

'Surely,' said the Princess.

So he climbed up to the window.

'Now,' said he, 'if I can do what your father asks, will
you marry me?'

'My father has promised that I shall,' said Melisande, playing with the white roses in her hand.

'Dear Princess,' said he, 'your father's promise is nothing to me. I want yours. Will you give it to me ?'

'Yes,' said she, and gave him the second rose.

'I want your hand.'

'Yes,' she said.

'And your heart with it.'

'Yes,' said the Princess, and she gave him the third rose.

'And a kiss to seal the promise.'

'Yes,' said she.

'And a kiss to go with the hand.'

'Yes,' she said.

'And a kiss to bring the heart.'

'Yes,' said the Princess, and she gave him the three kisses.

'Now,' said he, when he had given them back to her, 'to-night do not go to bed. Stay by your window, and I will stay down here in the garden and watch. And when your hair has grown to the filling of your room call to me, and then do as I tell you.'

'I will,' said the Princess.

So at dewy sunrise the Prince, lying on the turf beside the sun-dial, heard her voice—

'Florizel! Florizel! My hair has grown so long that it is pushing me out of the window.'

'Get out on to the window-sill,' said he, 'and twist your hair three times round the great iron hook that is there.'

And she did.

Then the Prince climbed up the rose bush with his naked sword in his teeth, and he took the Princess's hair in his hand about a yard from her head and said—

'Jump!'

The Princess jumped, and screamed, for there she was hanging from the hook by a yard and a half of her bright hair; the Prince tightened his grasp of the hair and drew his sword across it.

Then he let her down gently by her hair till her feet were on the grass, and jumped down after her.

They stayed talking in the garden till all the shadows had crept under their proper trees and the sun-dial said it was breakfast time.

Then they went in to breakfast, and all the Court crowded round to wonder and admire. For the Princess's hair had not grown.

'How did you do it?' asked the King, shaking Florizel warmly by the hand.

'The simplest thing in the world,' said Florizel, modestly. 'You have always cut the hair off the Princess. *I* just cut the Princess off the hair.'

'Humph!' said the King, who had a logical mind. And during breakfast he more than once looked anxiously at his daughter. When they got up from breakfast the Princess rose with the rest, but she rose and rose and rose, till it seemed as though there would never be an end of it. The Princess was nine feet high.

'I feared as much,' said the King, sadly. 'I wonder what will be the rate of progression. You see,' he said to poor Florizel, 'when we cut the hair off *it* grows—when we cut the Princess off *she* grows. I wish you had happened to think of that!'

The Princess went on growing. By dinner-time she was so large that she had to have her dinner brought out into the garden because she was too large to get indoors. But she was too unhappy to be able to eat anything. And she cried so much that there was quite a pool in the garden, and several pages were nearly drowned. So she remembered her 'Alice in Wonderland,' and stopped crying at once. But she did not stop growing. She grew bigger and bigger and bigger, till she had to go outside the palace gardens and sit on the common, and even that was too small to hold her comfortably, for every hour she grew twice as much as she had done the hour before. And nobody knew what to do, nor where the Princess was to sleep. Fortunately, her clothes had grown with her, or she would have been very cold indeed, and now she sat on the common in her green gown embroidered with gold, looking like a great hill covered with gorse in flower.

You cannot possibly imagine how large the Princess was growing, and her mother stood wringing her hands on the castle tower; and the Prince Florizel looked on broken-hearted to see his Princess snatched from his arms and turned into a lady as big as a mountain.

The King did not weep or look on. He sat down at once and wrote to his fairy godmother, asking her advice. He sent a weasel with the letter, and by return of weasel he got his own letter back again, marked 'Gone away. Left no address.'

It was now, when the kingdom was plunged into gloom, that a neighbouring King took it into his head to send an invading army against the island where Melisande lived. They came in ships and they landed in great numbers, and Melisande looking down from her height saw alien soldiers marching on the sacred soil of her country.

'I don't mind so much now,' said she, 'if I can really be of some use this size.'

And she picked up the army of the enemy in handfuls and double-handfuls, and put them back into their ships, and gave a little flip to each transport ship with her finger and thumb, which sent the ships off so fast that they never stopped till they reached their own country, and when they arrived there the whole army to a man said it would rather be court-martialled a hundred times over than go near the place again.

Meantime Melisande, sitting on the highest hill on the island, felt the land trembling and shivering under her giant feet.

'I do believe I'm getting too heavy,' she said, and jumped off the island into the sea, which was just up to her ankles. Just then a great fleet of warships and gunboats and torpedo boats came in sight, on their way to attack the island.

Melisande could easily have sunk them all with one kick, but she did not like to do this because it might have drowned the sailors, and besides, it might have swamped the island.

So she simply stooped and picked the island as you would pick a mushroom—for, of course, all islands are supported by a stalk underneath—and carried it away to another part of the world. So that when the warships got to where the island was marked on the map they found nothing but sea, and a very rough sea it was, because the Princess had churned it all up with her ankles as she walked away through it with the island.

When Melisande reached a suitable place, very sunny and warm, and with no sharks in the water, she set down the island; and the people made it fast with anchors, and then every one went to bed, thanking the kind fate which had sent them so great a Princess to help them in their need, and calling her the saviour of her country and the bulwark of the nation.

But it is poor work being the nation's bulwark and your country's saviour when you are miles high, and have no one to talk to, and when all you want is to be your humble right size again and to marry your sweetheart. And when it was dark the Princess came close to the island, and looked down, from far up, at her palace and her tower and cried, and cried, and cried. It does not matter how much you cry into the sea, it hardly makes any difference, however large you may be. Then when everything was quite dark the Princess looked up at the stars.

'I wonder how soon I shall be big enough to knock my head against them,' said she.

And as she stood star-gazing she heard a whisper right in her ear. A very little whisper, but quite plain.

'Cut off your hair!' it said.

Now, everything the Princess was wearing had grown big along with her, so that now there dangled from her golden girdle a pair of scissors as big as the Malay Peninsula, together with a pin-cushion the size of the Isle of Wight, and a yard measure that would have gone round Australia.

And when she heard the little, little voice, she knew it, small as it was, for the dear voice of Prince Florizel, and she whipped out the scissors from her gold case and snip, snip, snipped all her hair off, and it fell into the sea. The coral insects got hold of it at once and set to work on it, and now they have made it into the biggest coral reef in the world; but that has nothing to do with the story.

Then the voice said, 'Get close to the island,' and the Princess did, but she could not get very close because she was so large, and she looked up again at the stars and they seemed to be much farther off.

Then the voice said, 'Be ready to swim,' and she felt something climb out of her ear and clamber down her arm. The stars got farther and farther away, and next moment the Princess found herself swimming in the sea, and Prince Florizel swimming beside her.

'I crept on to your hand when you were carrying the island,' he explained, when their feet touched the sand and they walked in through the shallow water, 'and I got into your ear with an ear-trumpet. You never noticed me

because you were so great then.'

'Oh, my dear Prince,' cried Melisande, falling into his arms, 'you have saved me. I am my proper size again.'

So they went home and told the King and Queen. Both were very, very happy, but the King rubbed his chin with his hand, and said—

'You've certainly had some fun for your money, young man, but don't you see that we're just where we were before? Why, the child's hair is growing already.'

And indeed it was.

Then once more the King sent a letter to his godmother. He sent it by a flying-fish, and by return of fish came the answer—

'Just back from my holidays. Sorry for your troubles. Why not try scales?'

And on this message the whole Court pondered for hours.

But the Prince caused a pair of gold scales to be made, and hung them up in the palace gardens under a big oak tree. And the next morning he said to the Princess—

'My darling Melisande, I must really speak seriously to you. We are getting on in life. I am nearly twenty: it is

time that we thought of being settled. Will you trust me entirely and get into one of those gold scales?'

So he took her down into the garden, and helped her into the scale, and she curled up in it in her green and gold gown, like a little grass mound with buttercups on it.

'And what is going into the other scale?' asked Melisande.

'Your hair,' said Florizel. 'You see, when your hair is cut off you *it* grows, and when you are cut off your hair *you* grow—oh, my heart's delight, I can never forget how you grew, never! But if, when your hair is no more than you, and you are no more than your hair, I snip the scissors between you and it, then neither you nor your hair can possibly decide which ought to go on growing.'

'Suppose *both* did,' said the poor Princess, humbly.

'Impossible,' said the Prince, with a shudder; 'there are limits even to Malevola's malevolence. And, besides, Fortuna said "scales." Will you try it?'

'I will do whatever you wish,' said the poor Princess, 'but let me kiss my father and mother once, and Nurse, and you, too, my dear, in case I grow large again and can kiss nobody any more.'

So they came one by one and kissed the Princess.

Then the nurse cut off the Princess's hair, and at once it began to grow at a frightful rate.

The King and Queen and nurse busily packed it, as it grew, into the other scale, and gradually the scale went down a little. The Prince stood waiting between the scales with his drawn sword, and just before the two were equal he struck. But during the time his sword took to flash through the air the Princess's hair grew a yard or two, so that at the instant when he struck the balance was true.

'You are a young man of sound judgment,' said the King, embracing him, while the Queen and the nurse ran to help the Princess out of the gold scale.

The scale full of golden hair bumped down on to the ground as the Princess stepped out of the other one, and stood there before those who loved her, laughing and crying with happiness, because she remained her proper size, and her hair was not growing any more.

She kissed her Prince a hundred times, and the very next day they were married. Every one remarked on the beauty of the bride, and it was noticed that her hair was quite short—only five feet five and a quarter inches long—just down to her pretty ankles. Because the scales had been ten feet ten and a half inches apart, and the Prince, having a straight eye, had cut the golden hair exactly in the middle!

The Town in the Library
in the Town in the Library

The Town in the Library

Several points in this unusual story make it of special interest to Nesbit-readers. For one thing, Rosamund and Fabian were *real*; they were in fact the third and fourth of the five Bland children. E. N. was, as you know, Mrs Bland; she too comes into the tale, as you will see. Furthermore, the making of towns, scenes, cities from any objects to hand was very much a part of their childhood. It began when one of the little boys was trying to make an Indian fort out of building blocks and couldn't get the eastern atmosphere. His mother (who was also E. Nesbit), came to his aid and solved the problem with books, a few chessmen and a brass bowl upside down. Later, the Blands became very ambitious indeed in designing cities. Though *The Town in the Library* was one of E. Nesbit's earliest children's stories (it was written about the same time as the first Bastable books) the idea did not lie down. Out of it, rose her novel *The Magic City*, nearly a dozen years later, in 1910. Sadly, by this time Fabian had died very suddenly at the age of fifteen.

Meanwhile, in our story here, I very much like the piece of advice from the clockwork mouse, when the children want to know how to *leave* the town. 'It's a great secret,' he replies, 'but there is only one way out. You—I hardly know how to explain—you-you just *walk out of the gate*, you know.' But of course! Only, does one think of it?

N.L.

ROSAMUND AND FABIAN were left alone in the library.
You may not believe this; but I advise you to believe
everything I tell you, because it is true. Truth is stranger
than story-books, and when you grow up you will hear
people say this till you grow quite sick of listening to them:
you will then want to write the strangest story that ever was
—just to show that *some* stories can be stranger than truth.

Mother was obliged to leave the children alone, because
Nurse was ill with measles, which seems a babyish thing
for a grown-up nurse to have—but it is quite true. If I had
wanted to make up anything I could have said she was ill
of a broken heart or a brain-fever, which always happens
in books. But I wish to speak the truth even if it sounds
silly. And it *was* measles.

Mother could not stay with the children, because it was
Christmas Eve, and on that day a lot of poor old people
came up to get their Christmas presents, tea and snuff, and
flannel petticoats, and warm capes, and boxes of needles
and cottons and things like that. Generally the children
helped to give out the presents, but this year Mother was

afraid they might be going to have measles themselves, and measles is a nasty forward illness with no manners at all. You can catch it from a person before they know they've got it.

So the children were left alone. Before Mother went away she said—

'Look here, dears, you may play with your bricks, or make pictures with your pretty blocks that kind Uncle Thomas gave you, but you must not touch the two top-drawers of the bureau. Now don't forget. And if you're good you shall have tea with me, and perhaps there will be cake. Now you *will* be good, won't you?'

Fabian and Rosamund promised faithfully that they would be *very* good and that they would not touch the two top-drawers, and Mother went away to see about the flannel petticoats and the tea and snuff and tobacco and things. When the children were left alone, Fabian said—

'I am going to be very good. I shall be much more good than Mother expects me to.'

'We *won't* look in the drawers,' said Rosamund, stroking the shiny top of the bureau.

'We won't even *think* about the insides of the drawers,' said Fabian. He stroked the bureau too and his fingers left four long streaks on it, because he had been eating toffee.

'I suppose,' he said presently, 'we may open the two *bottom* drawers? Mother couldn't have made a mistake—could she?'

So they opened the two bottom drawers just to be sure that Mother hadn't made a mistake, and to see whether there was anything in the bottom drawers that they ought not to look at.

But the bottom drawer of all had only old magazines in

it. And the next to the bottom drawer had a lot of papers in it. The children knew at once by the look of the papers that they belonged to Father's great work about the Domestic Life of the Ancient Druids, and they knew it was not right—or even interesting—to try to read other people's papers.

So they shut the drawers and looked at each other, and Fabian said, 'I think it would be right to play with the bricks and the pretty blocks that Uncle Thomas gave us.'

But Rosamund was younger than Fabian, and she said, 'I am tired of the blocks, and I am tired of Uncle Thomas. I would rather look in the drawers.'

'So would I,' said Fabian. And they stood looking at the bureau.

Perhaps you don't know what a bureau is—children learn very little at school nowadays—so I will tell you that a bureau is a kind of chest of drawers. Sometimes it has a bookcase on the top of it, and instead of the two little top corner drawers like the chest of drawers in a bedroom it has a sloping lid, and when it is quite open you pull out two little boards underneath—and then it makes a sort of shelf for people to write letters on. The shelf lies quite flat, and lets you see little drawers inside with mother of pearl handles—and a row of pigeon holes—(which are not holes pigeons live in, but places for keeping the letters carrier-pigeons could carry round their necks if they liked). And there is very often a tiny cupboard in the middle of the bureau, with a pattern on the door in different coloured woods. So now you know.

Fabian stood first on one leg and then on the other, till Rosamund said—

'Well, you might as well pull up your socks.'

So he did. His socks were always just like a concertina or a very expensive photographic camera, but he used to say it was not his fault, and I suppose he knew best. Then he said—

'I say, Rom! Mother only said we weren't to *touch* the two top-drawers——'

'I *should* like to be good,' said Rosamund.

'I *mean* to be good,' said Fabian. 'But if you took the little thin poker that is not kept for best you could put it through one of the brass handles and I could hold the other handle with the tongs. And when we could open the drawer without touching it.'

'So we could! How clever you are, Fabe,' said Rosamund. And she admired her brother very much. So they took the poker and the tongs. The front of the bureau got a little scratched, but the top drawer came open, and there they saw two boxes with glass tops and narrow gold paper going all round; though you could only see paper shavings through the glass they knew it was soldiers. Besides these boxes there was a doll and a donkey standing on a green grass plot that had wooden wheels, and a little wicker-work

doll's cradle, and some brass cannons, and a bag that looked like marbles, and some flags, and a mouse that seemed as though it moved with clockwork; only, of course, they had promised not to touch the drawer, so they could not make sure. They looked at each other, and Fabian said:

'I wish it was to-morrow!'

You have seen that Fabian was quite a clever boy; and he knew at once that these were the Christmas presents which Santa Claus had brought for him and Rosamund. But Rosamund said, 'Oh dear, I wish we hadn't!'

However, she consented to open the other drawer—without touching it, of course, because she had promised faithfully—and when, with the poker and tongs, the other drawer came open, there were large wooden boxes—the kind that hold raisins and figs—and round boxes with paper on—smooth on the top and folded in pleats round the edge; and the children knew what was inside without looking. Every one knows what candied fruit looks like on the outside of the box. There were square boxes, too—the kind that have crackers in—with a cracker going off on the lid, very different in size and brightness from what it does really, for, as no doubt you know, a cracker very often comes in two quite calmly, without any pop at all, and then you only have the motto and the sweet, which is never nice. Of course, if there is anything else in the cracker, such as brooches or rings, you have to let the little girl who sits next to you at supper have it.

When they had pushed back the drawer Fabian said—

'Let us pull out the writing drawer and make a castle.'

So they pulled the drawer out and put it on the floor. Please do not try to do this if your father has a bureau, because it leads to trouble. It was only because this one was broken that they were able to do it.

Then they began to build. They had the two boxes of bricks—the wooden bricks with the pillars and the coloured glass windows, and the rational bricks which are made of clay like tiles. When all the bricks were used up they got the pretty picture blocks that kind Uncle Thomas gave them, and they built with these; but one box of blocks does not go far. Picture blocks are only good for building, except just at first. When you have made the pictures a few times you know exactly how they go, and then what's the good? This is a fault which belongs to many very expensive toys. These blocks had six pictures— Windsor Castle with the Royal Standard hoisted; ducks in a pond, with a very handsome green and blue drake; Rebecca at the well; a snowball fight—but none of the boys knew how to chuck a snowball; the Harvest Home; and the Death of Nelson.

These did not go far, as I said. There are six times as few blocks as there are pictures, because every block has six sides. If you don't understand this it shows they don't teach arithmetic at your school, or else that you don't do your home lessons.

But the best of a library is the books. Rosamund and Fabian made up with books. They got Shakespeare in fourteen volumes, and Rollin's *Ancient History* and Gibbon's *Decline and Fall*, and *The Beauties of Literature* in fifty-six fat little volumes, and they built not only a castle, but a town—and a big town—that presently towered high above them on the top of the bureau.

'It's almost big enough to get into,' said Fabian, 'if we had some steps.' So they made steps with the *British Essayists*, the *Spectator* and the *Rambler*, and the *Observer*, and the *Tatler*; and when the steps were done they walked up them.

You may think that they could not have walked up these steps and into a town they had built themselves, but I assure you people have often done it, and anyway this is a true story. They had made a lovely gateway with two fat volumes of Macaulay and Milton's poetical works on top, and as they went through it they felt all the feelings which people have to feel when they are tourists and see really fine architecture. (Architecture means buildings, but it is a grander word, as you see.)

Rosamund and Fabian simply walked up the steps into the town they had built. Whether they got larger or the town got smaller, I do not pretend to say. When they had gone under the great gateway they found that they were in a street which they could not remember building. But they were not disagreeable about it, and they said it was a very nice street all the same.

There was a large square in the middle of the town, with seats, and there they sat down, in the town they had made,

and wondered how they could have been so clever as to build it. Then they went to the walls of the town—high, strong walls built of the *Encyclopaedia* and the *Biographical Dictionary*—and far away over the brown plain of the carpet they saw a great thing like a square mountain. It was very shiny. And as they looked at it a great slice of it pushed itself out, and Fabian saw the brass handles shine, and he said:

'Why, Rom, that's the bureau.'

'It's larger than I want it to be,' said Rosamund, who was a little frightened. And indeed it did seem to be an extra size, for it was higher than the town.

The drawer of the great mountain bureau opened slowly, and the children could see something moving inside; then they saw the glass lid of one of the boxes go slowly up till it stood on end and looked like one side of the Crystal Palace, it was so large—and inside the box they saw something moving. The shavings and tissue-paper and the cotton-wool heaved and tossed like a sea when it is rough and you wish you had not come for a sail. And then from

among the heaving whiteness came out a blue soldier, and another and another. They let themselves down from the drawer with ropes of shavings, and when they were all out there were fifty of them—foot soldiers with rifles and fixed bayonets, as well as a thin captain on a horse and a sergeant and a drummer.

The drummer beat his drum and the whole company formed fours and marched straight for the town. They seemed to be quite full-size soldiers—indeed, *extra* large.

The children were very frightened. They left the walls and ran up and down the streets of the town trying to find a place to hide.

'Oh, there's our very own house,' cried Rosamund at last; 'we shall be safe there.' She was surprised as well as pleased to find their own house inside the town they had built.

So they ran in, and into the library, and there was the bureau and the town they had built, and it was all small and quite the proper size. But when they looked out of the window it was not their own street, but the one they had built; they could see two volumes of the *Beauties of Literature* and the head of Rebecca in the house opposite, and down the street was the Mausoleum they had built after the pattern given in the red and yellow book that went with the bricks. It was all very confusing.

Suddenly, as they stood looking out of the windows, they heard a shouting, and there were the blue soldiers coming along the street by twos, and when the Captain got opposite their house he called out—

'Fabian! Rosamund! come down!'

And they had to, for they were very much frightened.

Then the Captain said—

'We have taken this town, and you are our prisoners. Do not attempt to escape, or I don't know what will happen to you.'

The children explained that they had built the town, so they thought it was theirs; but the captain said very politely—

'That doesn't follow at all. It's our town now. And I want provisions for my soldiers.'

'We haven't any,' said Fabian, but Rosamund nudged him, and said, 'Won't the soldiers be very fierce if they are hungry?'

The Blue Captain heard her, and said—

'You are quite right, little girl. If you have any food, produce it. It will be a generous act, and may stop any unpleasantness. My soldiers *are* very fierce. Besides,' he added in a lower tone, speaking behind his hand, 'you need only feed the soldiers in the usual way.'

When the children heard this their minds were made up.

'If you do not mind waiting a minute,' said Fabian, politely, 'I will bring down any little things I can find.'

Then he took his tongs, and Rosamund took the poker, and they opened the drawer where the raisins and figs and dried fruits were—for everything in the library in the town was just the same as in the library at home—and they carried them out into the big square where the Captain had drawn up his blue regiment. And here the soldiers were fed. I suppose you know how tin soldiers are fed? But children learn so little at school nowadays that I daresay you don't, so I will tell you. You just put a bit of the fig or raisin, or whatever it is, on the soldier's tin bayonet—or his sword, if he is a cavalry man—and you let it stay on till you are tired of playing at giving the soldiers rations, and then of course *you eat it for him.* This was the way in which Fabian and Rosamund fed the starving blue soldiers. But when they had done so, the soldiers were as hungry as ever.

So then the Blue Captain, who had not had anything, even on the point of his sword, said—

'More—more, my gallant men are fainting for lack of food.'

So there was nothing for it but to bring out the candied fruits, and to feed the soldiers with them. So Fabian and

77

Rosamund stuck bits of candied apricot and fig and pear and cherry and beetroot on the tops of the soldiers' bayonets, and when every soldier had a piece they put a fat candied cherry on the officer's sword. Then the children knew the soldiers would be quiet for a few minutes, and they ran back into their own house and into the library to talk to each other about what they had better do, for they both felt that the blue soldiers were a very hard-hearted set of men.

'They might shut us up in the dungeons,' said Rosamund, 'and then Mother might lock us in, when she shut up the lid of the bureau, and we should starve to death.'

'I think it's all nonsense,' said Fabian. But when they looked out of the window there was the house with Windsor Castle and the head of Rebecca just opposite.

'If we could only find Mother,' said Rosamund; but they knew without looking that Mother was not in the house that they were in then.

'I wish we had that mouse that looked like clockwork—and the donkey, and the other box of soldiers—perhaps they are red ones, and they would fight the blue and lick them—because red-coats are English and they always win,' said Fabian.

And then Rosamund said—

'Oh, Fabe, I believe we could go into *this* town, too, if we tried!'

So they went to the bureau drawer, and Rosamund got out the other box of soldiers and the mouse—it *was* a clockwork one—and the donkey with panniers, and put them in the town, while Fabian ate up a few odd raisins that had dropped on the floor.

When all the soldiers (they *were* red) were arranged on

the ramparts of the little town, Fabian said—

'I'm sure we can get into this town,' and sure enough they did, just as they had done into the first one. And it was exactly the same sort of town as the other. So now they were in a town built in a library in a house in a town built in a library in a house in a town called London —and the town they were in now had red soldiers in it and they felt quite safe, and the Union Jack was stuck up over the gateway. It was a stiff little flag they had found with some others in the bureau drawer; it was meant to be stuck in the Christmas pudding, but they had stuck it between two blocks and put it over the gate of their town. They walked about this town and found their own house, just as before, and went in, and there was the toy town on the floor; and you will see that they might have walked into that town also, but they saw that it was no good, and that they couldn't get out that way, but would only get deeper and deeper into a nest of towns in libraries in houses in towns in libraries in houses in towns in . . . and so on for always—something like Chinese puzzle-boxes multiplied by millions and millions for ever and ever. And they did not like even to think of this, because of course they would be getting further and further from home every time. And when Fabian explained all this to Rosamund she said he made her head ache, and she began to cry.

Then Fabian thumped her on the back and told her not to be a little silly, for he was a very kind brother. And he said—

'Come out and let's see if the soldiers can tell us what to do.'

So they went out; but the red soldiers said they knew nothing but drill, and even the Red Captain said he really

couldn't advise. Then they met the clockwork mouse. He was big like an elephant, and the donkey with panniers was as big as a mastodon or a megatherium. (If they teach you anything at school of course they have taught you all about the megatherium and the mastodon.)

The Mouse kindly stopped to speak to the children, and Rosamund burst into tears again and said she wanted to go home.

The great Mouse looked down at her and said—

'I am sorry for *you*, but your brother is the kind of child that overwinds clockwork mice the very first day he has them. I prefer to stay this size, and you to stay small.'

Then Fabian said: 'On my honour, I won't. If we get back home I'll give you to Rosamund. That is, supposing I get you for one of my Christmas presents.'

The donkey with panniers said—

'And you won't put coals in my panniers or unglue my

feet from my green grass-plot because I look more natural without wheels?'

'I give you my word,' said Fabian, 'I wouldn't think of such a thing.'

'Very well,' said the Mouse, 'then I will tell you. It is a great secret, but there is only one way to get out of this kind of town. You—I hardly know how to explain—you—you just *walk out of the gate*, you know.'

'Dear me,' said Rosamund; 'I never thought of that!'

So they all went to the gate of the town and walked out, and there they were in the library again. But when they looked out of the window the Mausoleum was still to be seen, and the terrible blue soldiers.

'What are we to do now?' asked Rosamund; but the clockwork mouse and the donkey with panniers were their proper size again now (or else the children had got bigger. It is no use asking me which, for I do not know), and so of course they could not speak.

'We must walk out of this town as we did out of the other,' said Fabian.

'Yes,' Rosamund said; 'only this town is full of blue

soldiers and I am afraid of them. Don't you think it would do if we *ran* out?'

So out they ran and down the steps that were made of the *Spectator* and the *Rambler* and the *Tatler* and the *Observer*. And directly they stood on the brown library carpet they ran to the window and looked out, and they saw—instead of the building with Windsor Castle and Rebecca's head in it,—they saw their own road with the trees without any leaves and the man was just going along lighting the lamps with the stick that the gas-light pops out of, like a bird, to roost in the glass cage at the top of the lamp-post. So they knew that they were safe at home again.

And as they stood looking out they heard the library door open, and Mother's voice saying—

'What a dreadful muddle! And what have you done with the raisins and the candied fruits?' And her voice was very grave indeed.

Now you will see that it was quite impossible for Fabian

and Rosamund to explain to their mother what they had done with the raisins and things, and how they had been in a town in a library in a house in a town they had built in their own library with the books and the bricks and the pretty picture blocks kind Uncle Thomas gave them. Because they were much younger than I am, and even I have found it rather hard to explain.

So Rosamund said, 'Oh, Mother, my head does ache so,' and began to cry. And Fabian said nothing, but he, also, began to cry.

And Mother said, 'I don't wonder your head aches, after all those sweet things.' And she looked as if she would like to cry too.

'I don't know what Daddy will say,' said Mother, and then she gave them each a nasty powder and put them both to bed.

'I wonder what he *will* say,' said Fabian just before he went to sleep.

SPECTATOR
THE RAMBLER
TATLER

'*I* don't know,' said Rosamund, and, strange to say, they don't know to this hour what Daddy said. Because next day they both had measles, and when they got better every one had forgotten about what had happened on Christmas Eve. And Fabian and Rosamund had forgotten just as much as everybody else. So I should never have heard of it but for the clockwork mouse. It was he who told me the story, just as the children told it to him in the town in the library in the house in the town they built in their own library with the books and the bricks and the pretty picture blocks which were given to them by kind Uncle Thomas. And if you do not believe the story it is not my fault: I believe every word the mouse said, for I know the good character of that clockwork mouse, and I know it could not tell an untruth even if it tried.

Belinda and Bellamant
or the Bells of Carillon-Land

Belinda and Bellamant

This was one of the last of E. Nesbit's fairy tales. But you can see the special Nesbit touch in that *Royal Match Catalogue Illustrated*—('Prince B, aged 24, wants Princess who doesn't object to christening curse. Nature of curse only revealed in the strictest confidence'). What may seem puzzling to most of us now is the bell that 'doesn't ring, can't ring and wasn't made to ring'. Yet a diving-bell (which it was) has a very long history. In fact, it was 'modernized' and made more practical some two hundred years ago by John Smeaton (1724–94) who—among other achievements—built the third and best Eddystone Lighthouse. You can find a diving-bell now and then in adventure stories. There is a form of it in Verne's *Twenty Thousand Leagues Under the Sea* (1870 in the original French). To see how it works, more or less, turn a glass or bowl upside down and push it under water. Part of the inside will (or should), stay dry.

N.L.

THERE IS A CERTAIN COUNTRY where a king is never allowed to reign while a queen can be found. They like queens much better than kings in that country. I can't think why. If some one has tried to teach you a little history, you will perhaps think that this is the Salic law. But it isn't. In the biggest city of that odd country there is a great bell-tower (higher than the clock-tower of the Houses of Parliament, where they put M.P.'s who forget their manners). This bell-tower had seven bells in it, very sweet-toned splendid bells, made expressly to ring on the joyful occasions when a princess was born who would be queen some day. And the great tower was built expressly for the bells to ring in. So you see what a lot they thought of queens in that country. Now in all the bells there are Bell-people—it is their voices that you hear when the bells ring. All that about its being the clapper of the bell is mere nonsense, and would hardly deceive a child. I don't know why people say such things. Most Bell-people are very energetic and busy. They love the sound of their own voices, and hate being idle, and when nearly two hundred years had gone by, and no princesses had been born, they

87

got tired of living in bells that were never rung. So they slipped out of the belfry one fine frosty night, and left the big beautiful bells empty, and went off to find other homes. One of them went to live in a dinner-bell, and one in a school-bell, and the rest all found homes—they did not mind where—just anywhere, in fact, where they could find any Bell-person kind enough to give them board and lodging. And every one was surprised at the increased loudness in the voices of these hospitable bells. For, of course, the Bell-people from the belfry did their best to help in the housework as polite guests should, and always added their voices to those of their hosts on all occasions when bell-talk was called for. And the seven big beautiful bells in the belfry were left hollow and dark and quite empty, except for the the clappers who did not care about the comforts of a home.

Now of course a good house does not remain empty long, especially when there is no rent to pay, and in a very short time the seven bells all had tenants, and they were all the kind of folk that no respectable Bell-people would care to be acquainted with.

They had been turned out of other bells—cracked bells and broken bells, the bells of horses that had been lost in snowstorms or of ships that had gone down at sea. They hated work, and they were a glum, silent, disagreeable people, but as far as they could be pleased about anything they were pleased to live in bells that were never rung, in houses where there was nothing to do. They sat hunched up under the black domes of their houses, dressed in darkness and cobwebs, and their only pleasure was idleness, their only feasts the thick dusty silence that lies heavy in all belfries where the bells never ring. They hardly ever spoke even to each other, and then it was in the whispers that Bell-people talk in among themselves; and that no one can hear but the bat whose ear for music is very fine and who has himself a particularly high voice; and when they did speak they quarrelled.

And when at last the bells *were* rung for the birth of a Princess the wicked Bell-people were furious. Of course they had to *ring*—a bell can't help that when the rope is pulled—but their voices were so ugly that people were quite shocked.

'What poor taste our ancestors must have had,' they said, 'to think these were good bells!'

(You remember the bells had not rung for nearly two hundred years.)

'Dear me,' said the King to the Queen, 'what odd ideas people had in the old days. I always understood that these bells had beautiful voices.'

'They're quite hideous,' said the Queen. And so they were. Now that night, the lazy Bell-folk came down out of the belfry full of anger against the Princess whose birth had disturbed their idleness. There is no anger like that of a lazy person who is made to work against his will.

And they crept out of the dark domes of their houses and came down in their dust dresses and cobweb cloaks, and crept up to the palace where every one had gone to bed long before, and stood round the mother-of-pearl cradle where the baby princess lay asleep. And they reached their seven dark right hands out across the white satin coverlet, and the oldest and hoarsest and laziest said:

'She shall grow uglier every day, except Sundays, and every Sunday she shall be seven times prettier than the Sunday before.'

'Why not uglier every day, and a double dose on Sunday?' asked the youngest and spitefullest of the wicked Bell-people.

'Because there's no rule without an exception,' said the eldest and hoarsest and laziest, 'and she'll feel it all the more if she's pretty once a week. And,' he added, 'this shall go on till she finds a bell that doesn't ring, and can't ring, and never will ring, and wasn't made to ring.'

'Why not for ever?' asked the young and spiteful.

'Nothing goes on for ever,' said the eldest Bell-person, 'not even ill-luck. And we have to leave her a way out. It doesn't matter. She'll never know what it is. Let alone finding it.'

Then they went back to the belfry and rearranged as well as they could the comfortable web-and-owls' nest furniture of their houses which had all been shaken up and disarranged by that absurd ringing of bells at the birth of a Princess that nobody could really be pleased about.

When the Princess was two weeks old the King said to the Queen:

'My love—the Princess is not so handsome as I thought she was.'

'Nonsense, Henry,' said the Queen, 'the light's not good, that's all.'

Next day—it was Sunday—the King pulled back the lace curtains of the cradle and said:

'The light's good enough now—and you see she's——'

He stopped.

'It *must* have been the light,' he said, 'she looks all right to-day.'

'Of course she does, a precious,' said the Queen.

But on Monday morning His Majesty was quite sure

really that the Princess was rather plain, for a Princess. And when Sunday came, and the Princess had on her best robe and the cap with the little white ribbons in the frill, he rubbed his nose and said there was no doubt dress did make a great deal of difference. For the Princess was now as pretty as a new daisy.

The Princess was several years old before her mother could be got to see that it really was better for the child to wear plain clothes and a veil on week days. On Sundays, of course she could wear her best frock and a clean crown just like anybody else.

Of course nobody ever told the Princess how ugly she was. She wore a veil on week-days, and so did every one else in the palace, and she was never allowed to look in the glass except on Sundays, so that she had no idea that she was not as pretty all the week as she was on the first day of it. She grew up therefore quite contented. But the parents were in despair.

'Because,' said King Henry, 'it's high time she was married. We ought to choose a king to rule the realm—I

have always looked forward to her marrying at twenty-one
—and to our retiring on a modest competence to some nice
little place in the country where we could have a few pigs.'

'And a cow,' said the Queen, wiping her eyes.

'And a pony and trap,' said the King.

'And hens,' said the Queen, 'yes. And now it can never,
never be. Look at the child! I just ask you! Look at her!'

'*No*,' said the King firmly, 'I haven't done that since she
was ten, except on Sundays.'

'Couldn't we get a prince to agree to a "Sundays only"
marriage—not let him see her during the week?'

'Such an unusual arrangement,' said the King, 'would
involve very awkward explanations, and I can't think of
any except the true ones, which would be quite impossible
to give. You see, we should want a first-class prince, and
no really high-toned Highness would take a wife on those
terms.'

'It's a thoroughly comfortable kingdom,' said the Queen
doubtfully. 'The young man would be handsomely provided for for life.'

'I couldn't marry Belinda to a time-server or a place-
worshipper,' said the King decidedly.

Meanwhile the Princess had taken the matter into her
own hands. She had fallen in love.

You know, of course, that a handsome book is sent out
every year to all the kings who have daughters to marry.
It is rather like the illustrated catalogues of Liberty's or
Peter Robinson's, only instead of illustrations showing
furniture or ladies' cloaks and dresses, the pictures are all
of princes who are of an age to be married, and are looking
out for suitable wives. The book is called the *Royal Match
Catalogue Illustrated*,—and besides the pictures of the

princes it has little printed bits about their incomes, accomplishments, prospects, tempers and relations.

Now the Princess saw this book—which is never shown to princesses, but only to their parents—when it was carelessly left lying on the round table in the parlour. She looked all through it, and she hated each prince more than the one before till she came to the very end, and on the last page of all, screwed away in a corner, was the picture of a prince who was quite as good-looking as a prince has any call to be.

'I like *you*,' said Belinda softly. Then she read the little bit of print underneath.

Prince Bellamant, aged twenty-four. Wants Princess who doesn't object to a christening curse. Nature of curse only revealed in the strictest confidence. Good tempered. Comfortably off. Quiet habits. No relations.

'Poor dear,' said the Princess. 'I wonder what the curse is! I'm sure *I* shouldn't mind!'

The blue dusk of evening was deepening in the garden outside. The Princess rang for the lamp and went to draw the curtain. There was a rustle and a faint high squeak— and something black flopped fluttering on to the floor.

'Oh—it's a bat,' cried the Princess, as the lamp came in. 'I don't like bats.'

'Let me fetch a dust-pan and brush and sweep the nasty thing away,' said the parlour-maid.

'No, no,' said Belinda, 'it's hurt, poor dear,' and though she hated bats she picked it up. It was horribly cold to touch, and one wing dragged loosely. 'You can go, Jane,' said the Princess to the parlour-maid.

Then she got a big velvet-covered box that had had chocolate in it, and put some cotton wool in it and said to the Bat—

'You poor dear, is that comfortable?' and the Bat said: 'Quite, thanks.'

'Good gracious,' said the Princess jumping. 'I didn't know bats could talk.'

'Every one can talk,' said the Bat, 'but not every one can hear other people talking. You have a fine ear as well as a fine heart.'

'Will your wing ever get well?' asked the Princess.

'I hope so,' said the Bat. 'But let's talk about you. Do you know why you wear a veil every day except Sundays?'

'Doesn't everybody?' asked Belinda.

'Only here in the palace,' said the Bat, 'that's on your account.'

'But why?' asked the Princess.

'Look in the glass and you'll know.'

'But it's wicked to look in the glass except on Sundays— and besides they're all put away,' said the Princess.

'If I were you,' said the Bat, 'I should go up into the attic where the youngest kitchen-maid sleeps. Feel between the thatch and the wall just above her pillow, and you'll find a little round looking-glass. But come back here before you look at it.'

The Princess did exactly what the Bat told her to do, and when she had come back into the parlour and shut the door she looked in the little round glass that the youngest kitchen-maid's sweetheart had given her. And when she saw her ugly, ugly, ugly face—for you must remember she had been growing uglier every day since she was born—she screamed and then she said:

'That's not me, it's a horrid picture.'

'It *is* you, though,' said the Bat firmly but kindly; 'and now you see why you wear a veil all the week—and only look in the glass on Sunday.'

'But why,' asked the Princess in tears, 'why don't I look like that in the Sunday looking-glasses?'

'Because you aren't like that on Sundays,' the Bat replied. 'Come,' it went on, 'stop crying. I didn't tell you the dread secret of your ugliness just to make you cry—but because I know the way for you to be as pretty all the week as you are on Sundays, and since you've been so kind to me I'll tell you. Sit down.'

The Princess did, and listened through her veil and her tears, while the Bat told her all that I began this story by telling you.

'My great-great-great-great-grandfather heard the tale years ago,' he said, 'up in the dark, dusty, beautiful, comfortable, cobwebby belfry, and I have heard scraps of it myself when the evil Bell-people were quarrelling, or talking in their sleep, lazy things!'

'It's very good of you to tell me all this,' said Belinda, 'but what am I to do?'

'You must find the bell that doesn't ring, and can't ring, and never will ring, and wasn't made to ring.'

'If I were a prince,' said the Princess, 'I could go out and seek my fortune.'

'Princesses have fortunes as well as princes,' said the Bat.

'But father and mother would never let me go and look for mine.'

'Think!' said the Bat, 'perhaps you'll find a way.'

So Belinda thought and thought. And at last she got the book that had the portraits of eligible princes in it, and she wrote to the prince who had the christening curse—and this is what she said:

'Princess Belinda of Carillon-land is not afraid of christening curses. If Prince Bellamant would like to marry her he had better apply to her Royal Father in the usual way.

'P.S.—I have seen your portrait.'

When the Prince got this letter he was very pleased, and wrote at once for Princess Belinda's likeness. Of course they sent him a picture of her Sunday face, which was the most beautiful face in the world. As soon as he saw it he knew that this was not only the most beautiful face in the world, but the dearest, so he wrote to her father by the next post—applying for her hand in the usual way and enclosing the most respectable references. The King told the Princess.

'Come,' said he, 'what do you say to this young man?'

And the Princess, of course, said, 'Yes, please.'

So the wedding-day was fixed for the first Sunday in June.

But when the Prince arrived with all his glorious following of courtiers and men-at-arms, with two pink peacocks and a crown-case full of diamonds for his bride, he absolutely refused to be married on a Sunday. Nor would he give any reason for his refusal. And then the King lost his temper and broke off the match, and the Prince went away.

But he did not go very far. That night he bribed a page-boy to show him which was the Princess's room, and he climbed up by the jasmine through the dark rose-scented night, and tapped at the window.

'Who's dhere?' said the Princess inside in the dark.

'Me,' said the Prince in the dark outside.

'Thed id wasnd't true?' said the Princess. 'They toad be you'd ridded away.'

'What a cold you've got, my Princess,' said the Prince hanging on by the jasmine boughs.

'It's not a cold,' sniffed the Princess.

'Then . . . oh you dear . . . were you crying because you thought I'd gone?' he said.

'I suppose so,' said she.

He said, 'You dear!' again, and kissed her hands.

'*Why* wouldn't you be married on a Sunday?' she asked.

'It's the curse, dearest,' he explained, 'I couldn't tell any one but you. The fact is, Malevola wasn't asked to my christening so she doomed me to be . . . well, she said "moderately good-looking all the week, and too ugly for words on Sundays." So you see! You *will* be married on a week-day, won't you ?'

'But I can't,' said the Princess, 'because I've got a curse too—only I'm ugly all the week and pretty on Sundays.'

'How extremely tiresome,' said the Prince, 'but can't you be cured ?'

'Oh yes,' said the Princess, and told him how. 'And you,' she asked, 'is yours quite incurable ?'

'Not at all,' he answered, 'I've only got to stay under water for five minutes and the spell will be broken. But you see, beloved, the difficulty is that I can't do it. I've practised regularly, from a boy, in the sea, and in the swimming bath, and even in my wash-hand basin—hours at a time I've practised—but I never can keep under more than two minutes.'

'Oh dear,' said the Princess, 'this is dreadful.'

'It is rather trying,' the Prince answered.

'You're sure you like me,' she asked suddenly, 'now you know that I'm only pretty once a week?'

'I'd die for you,' said he.

'Then I'll tell you what. Send all your courtiers away, and take a situation as under-gardener here—I know we want one. And then every night I'll climb down the jasmine and we'll go out together and seek our fortune. I'm sure we shall find it.'

And they did go out. The very next night, and the next, and the next, and the next, and the next, and the next. And they did not find their fortunes, but they got fonder and fonder of each other. They could not see each other's faces, but they held hands as they went along through the dark.

And on the seventh night, as they passed by a house that showed chinks of light through its shutters, they heard a bell being rung outside for supper, a bell with a very loud and beautiful voice. But instead of saying—

'Supper's ready,' as any one would have expected, the bell was saying—

> Ding dong dell!
> *I* could tell
> Where you ought to go
> To break the spell.

Then some one left off ringing the bell, so of course it couldn't say any more. So the two went on. A little way down the road a cow-bell tinkled behind the wet hedge of the lane. And it said—not, 'Here I am, quite safe,' as a cow-bell should, but—

> Ding dong dell
> All will be well
> If you . . .

99

Then the cow stopped walking and began to eat, so the bell couldn't say any more. The Prince and Princess went on, and you will not be surprised to hear that they heard the voices of five more bells that night. The next was a school-bell. The schoolmaster's little boy thought it would be fun to ring it very late at night—but his father came and caught him before the bell could say any more than—

> Ding a dong dell
> You can break up the spell
> By taking . . .

So that was no good.

Then there were the three bells that were the sign over the door of an inn where people were happily dancing to a fiddle, because there was a wedding. These bells said:

> We are the
> Merry three
> Bells, bells, bells.
> You are two
> To undo
> Spells, spells, spells . . .

Then the wind who was swinging the bells suddenly thought of an appointment he had made with a pine forest to get up an entertaining imitation of sea-waves for the benefit of the forest nymphs who had never been to the seaside, and he went off—so, of course, the bells couldn't ring any more, and the Prince and Princess went on down the dark road.

There was a cottage and the Princess pulled her veil closely over her face, for yellow light streamed from its open door—and it was a Wednesday.

Inside a little boy was sitting on the floor—quite a little boy—he ought to have been in bed long before, and I don't know why he wasn't. And he was ringing a little tinkling bell that had dropped off a sleigh.

And this little bell said:

Tinkle, tinkle, tinkle, I'm a little sleigh-bell,
But I know what I know, and I'll tell, tell, tell.
Find the Enchanter of the Ringing Well,
He will show you how to break the spell, spell, spell.
Tinkle, tinkle, I'm a little sleigh-bell,
But I know what I know. . . .

And so on, over and over, again and again, because the little boy was quite contented to go on shaking his sleigh-bell for ever and ever.

'So now we know,' said the Prince, 'isn't that glorious?'

'Yes, very, but where's the Enchanter of the Ringing Well?' said the Princess doubtfully.

'Oh, I've got *his* address in my pocket-book,' said the Prince. 'He's my god-father. He was one of the references I gave your father.'

So the next night the Prince brought a horse to the garden, and he and the Princess mounted, and rode, and rode, and rode, and in the grey dawn they came to Wonderwood, and in the very middle of that the Enchanter's Palace stands.

The Princess did not like to call on a perfect stranger so very early in the morning, so they decided to wait a little and look about them.

The castle was very beautiful, decorated with a conventional design of bells and bell ropes, carved in stone.

Luxuriant plants of American bell-vine covered the drawbridge and portcullis. On a green lawn in front of the castle was a well, with a curious bell-shaped covering suspended over it. The lovers leaned over the mossy fern-grown wall of the well, and, looking down, they could see that the narrowness of the well only lasted for a few feet, and below that it spread into a cavern where water lay in a big pool.

'What cheer?' said a pleasant voice behind them. It was the Enchanter, an early riser, like Darwin was, and all other great scientific men.

They told him what cheer.

'But,' Prince Bellamant ended, 'it's really no use. I can't keep under water more than two minutes however much I try. And my precious Belinda's not likely to find any silly old bell that doesn't ring, and can't ring, and never will ring, and was never made to ring.'

'Ho, ho,' laughed the Enchanter with the soft full laughter of old age. 'You've come to the right shop. Who told you?'

'The bells,' said Belinda.

'Ah, yes.' The old man frowned kindly upon them. 'You must be very fond of each other?'

'We are,' said the two together.

'Yes,' the Enchanter answered, 'because only true lovers can hear the true speech of the bells, and then only when they're together. Well, there's the bell!'

He pointed to the covering of the well, went forward, and touched some lever or spring. The covering swung out from above the well, and hung over the grass grey with the dew of dawn.

'*That?*' said Bellamant.

'That,' said his god-father, 'is what's called a diving bell. It doesn't ring, and it can't ring, and it never will ring, and it was never made to ring. Get into it.'

'Eh ?' said Bellamant forgetting his manners.

The old man took a hand of each and led them under the bell.

They looked up. It had windows of thick glass, and high seats about four feet from its edge, running all round inside.

'Take your seats,' said the Enchanter.

Bellamant lifted his Princess to the bench and leaped up beside her.

'Now,' said the old man, 'sit still, hold each other's hands, and for your lives don't move.'

He went away, and next moment they felt the bell swing in the air. It swung round till once more it was over the well, and then it went down, down, down.

'I'm not afraid, with you,' said Belinda, because she was, dreadfully.

Down went the bell. The glass windows leaped into light, and looking through them, the two could see blurred glories of lamps in the side of the well. Then with a plop the lower edge of the bell met the water, the water rose inside it, a little, then not any more. And the bell went down, down, and above their heads the green water lapped against the windows of the bell.

'You're under water—if we stay five minutes,' Belinda whispered.

'Yes, dear,' said Bellamant, and pulled out his ruby-studded chronometer.

'It's five minutes for you, but oh!' cried Belinda, 'it's *now* for me. For I've found the bell that doesn't ring, and can't ring, and never will ring, and wasn't made to ring. Oh Bellamant dearest, it's Thursday. *Have* I got my Sunday face?'

She tore away her veil, and his eyes, fixed upon her face, could not leave it.

'Oh dream of all the world's delight,' he murmured, 'how beautiful you are.'

Neither spoke again till a sudden little shock told them that the bell was moving up again.

'Nonsense,' said Bellamant, 'it's not five minutes.'

But when they looked at the ruby-studded chronometer, it was nearly three-quarters of an hour. But then, of course, the well was enchanted.

'Magic? Nonsense,' said the old man when they hung about him with thanks and pretty words. 'As I told you, it's only a diving-bell.'

* * *

So they went home and were married, and the Princess did not wear a veil at the wedding. She said she had had enough veils to last her a life time.

* * *

And a year and a day after that a little daughter was born to them.

'Now sweetheart,' said King Bellamant—he was king now because the old king and queen had retired from the business, and were keeping pigs and hens in the country

as they had always planned to do—'I am going to ring the bells with my own hands, to show how glad I am for you, and for the child, and for our good life together.'

So he went out. It was very dark, because the baby princess had chosen to be born at midnight.

The King went out to the belfry, that stood in the great, bare, quiet, moonlit square, and he opened the door. The furry-pussy bell-ropes, like huge caterpillars, hung on the first loft. The King began to climb the curly-wurly stone stair. And as he went up he heard a noise, the strangest noises, stamping and rustling and deep breathings.

He stood still in the ringers' loft where the pussy-furry caterpillary bell-ropes hung, and from the belfry above he heard the noise of strong fighting, and mixed with it the sound of voices angry and desperate, but with a noble note that thrilled the soul of the hearer like the sound of the trumpet in battle. And the voices cried:

> Down, down—away, away,
> When good has come ill may not stay,
> Out, out, into the night,
> The belfry bells are ours by right!

And the words broke and joined again, like water when it flows against the piers of a bridge. 'Down, down——.' 'Ill may not stay——.' 'Good has come——.' 'Away, away ——.' And the joining came like the sound of the river that flows free again.

> Out, out, into the night,
> The belfry bells are ours by right!

And then, as King Bellamant stood there, thrilled and yet, as it were, turned to stone, by the magic of this conflict that raged above him, there came a sweeping rush down the belfry ladder. The lantern he carried showed him a rout of little, dark, evil people, clothed in dust and cobwebs, that scurried down the wooden steps gnashing their

teeth and growling in the bitterness of a deserved defeat.
They passed and there was silence. Then the King flew
from rope to rope pulling lustily, and from above, the bells
answered in their own clear beautiful voices—because the
good Bell-people had driven out the usurpers and had
come to their own again.

> Ring-a-ring-a-ring-a-ring-a-ring! Ring, bell!
> A little baby comes on earth to dwell. Ring, bell!
> Sound, bell! Sound! Swell!
> Ring for joy and wish her well!
> May her life tell
> No tale of ill-spell!
> Ring, bell! Joy, bell!
> Ring!

The White Horse

The White Horse

Kent was E. Nesbit's county, the place of nearly all her favourite homes throughout her life (*see* Introduction). And it is surely the setting of this summery story with its apple orchard, its farms and fields, its White Horse (described in the last paragraph)—and, if we need another clue, the Apple Door, 'spelt differently'. That is of course Appledore; you can find it on the map of Kent, and a very nice place too. Alert readers will notice that the number of wish-apples used and the number left don't seem to follow the rules of normal arithmetic. There is no need to worry; it is simply a fine example of the special mathematics of fairy tale.

N.L.

'PLEASE, FATHER,' Diggory said, 'I want to go out and seek my fortune.'

'Seek your grandmother,' said his father, but not unkindly. He was smoking a pipe outside his cottage door, and he had a red-spotted handkerchief over his head because of the flies. There were flies then, just the same as there are now, though it was a hundred years ago by the church clock.

'I wasn't thinking of my grandmother,' said Diggory; 'I was thinking of my Uncle Diggory. He was the third son of a woodcutter, just like I am, and he saw right enough that that's the sort that *has* to go out and seek its fortune. and I'm getting on, father; I shall be twenty before you know where you are.'

'You'll have to be twenty and more before I agree not to know where *you* are,' said his father. 'Your Uncle Diggory did well for himself, sure enough, and many a turkey and chine he's sent us at Christmas-time; but he started a-horseback, he did. He got the horse from *his* Uncle Diggory, and he was a rover too. Now, if you went, you'd have to go on Shank's mare, and them that go a-foot comes back a-foot.'

'Will you let me go, then, if I can get a horse?' said Diggory coaxingly. 'Do say yes, dad, and then I won't say another word about it till I've got the horse.'

'Drat the lad—*yes*, then!' shouted the father.

Diggory jumped up from the porch seat.

'Then farewell home and hey for the road,' cried he, 'for I've got the horse, dad. My Uncle Diggory sent it to me this very day, and it's tied up behind the lodge; white it is, and a red saddle and bridle fit for a King.'

The woodcutter grumbled, but he was a woodcutter of honour, and having said 'Yes,' he had to stick to yes.

So Diggory rode off on the white horse with the scarlet saddle, and all the village turned out to see him go. He had on his best white smock, and he had never felt so fine in all his days.

So he rode away. When he came to the Round Mound windmill he stopped, for there was Joyce taking in the clean clothes from the hedge, because it was Monday evening.

He told her where he was going.

'You might take me with you,' she said. 'I'm not so very heavy but what we could both ride on that great big horse of yours.' And she held up a face as sweet as a bunch of flowers.

But Diggory said, 'No, my dear. Why, you little silly, girls can't go to seek their fortunes. You'd only be in my way! Wish me luck, child.'

So he rode on, and she folded up the linen all crooked, and damped it down with her tears, so that it was quite ready for ironing.

Diggory rode on, and on, and on. He rode through dewy evening, and through the cool black night, and right into the fresh-scented pinky pearly dawning. And when it was real live wide-awake morning, Diggory felt very thin and empty inside his smock, and he remembered that he had had nothing to eat since dinner-time yesterday, and then it was pork and greens.

He rode on, and he rode on, and by-and-by he came to a red brick wall, very strong and stout, with big buttresses and a stone coping. His horse (whom he had christened Invicta, although you might have called him something different) was a very high horse indeed, and by standing up in his stirrups Diggory could see over the wall. And he saw that on the other side was an orchard full of trees full of apples, red, and yellow, and green. He reined Invicta in close under the wall and said, 'Woa, there! stand still, will 'e ?' And he stood up on the broad saddle and made a jump and caught at the stone coping of the wall, and next moment he had hung by his hands and dropped into the orchard. And it was a very long drop indeed. For he had quite made up his mind to take some of the apples. First, because he was hungry, and, secondly, because boys *will* take apples—in stories that is, of course; *really*, they would never think of such a thing.

With a practised eye, Diggory chose the tree with the fattest, rosiest apples on it. He climbed the tree, and had just settled himself astride a convenient bough when he heard a voice say: 'Hi! You up there!'

And, looking down, he saw a flat-faced old man with a red flannel waistcoat standing under the tree looking up spitefully.

'Good-morning, my fine fellow,' said the old man. 'You seem a nice honest lad, and I'm sorry for your sake that apple stealing's punished so severely in these parts.'

'I've not had any apples yet,' said Diggory. 'Look here,

I'll go away if you like, and we'll say no more about it.'

'That's a handsome offer, very,' said the nasty old man; 'but this is an enchanted orchard, and you can't go away without with your leave or by your leave, as you came in. Why, you can't even get out of the tree—and as for climbing the wall, no one can do it without a white horse to help him. So now where are you?'

Diggory knew very well where he was, and he tried at once to be somewhere else, but the old man was right. He could move all about the tree from branch to branch, but the tree felt wrong way up and he felt wrong way up; that is to say, he could not get to the ground except by jumping much harder than he knew how to, and then he knew he would only have fallen back again, just as you would fall back if you jumped up to the ceiling. He could have fallen off the tree the other way, of course, but then he would have fallen up into the sky, and there seemed to be nothing

there to stop his falling for ever and ever. So he held tight and looked at the old man. And Diggory thought he looked nastier than ever.

So he said: 'Well?'

And the old man said: 'Not at all! However, since you had the sense not to fall off wrong way, I suppose you're the boy I want. Now, look here, you throw me down those ten big apples, one by one, so that I can catch them, and I'll let you go out by the Apple Door that no one but me has the key of.'

'Why don't you pick them yourself?' Diggory asked.

'I'm too old; you know very well that old men don't climb trees. Come, is it a bargain?'

'I don't know,' said the boy; 'there are lots of apples you can reach without climbing. Why do you want these so particularly?'

As he spoke, he picked one of the apples and threw it up and caught it. I say up, but it was down instead, because of the apple-tree being so very much enchanted.

'Oh, *don't!*' the old man squeaked like a rat in a trap—'*don't* drop it! Throw it down to me, you nasty slack-backed, smock-frocked son of a speckled toad!'

Diggory's blood boiled at hearing his father called a toad.

'Take that!' cried he, aiming the apple at the old man's head. 'I wish I could get out of this tree.'

The apple hit the old man's head and bounced on to the grass, and the moment that apple touched the ground Diggory found that he *could* get out of the tree if he liked, for he felt that he was now the proper way up once more, and so was the tree.

'So,' he said, 'these are wish-apples, are they?'

'No, no, no, no!' shrieked the old man so earnestly that Diggory knew he was lying. 'I've just disenchanted you, that's all. You see, most people fall up out of the tree and you didn't, so I thought I'd let you go, because I'm a nice kind old man, I am, and I wouldn't so much as hurt a fly. They aren't wish-apples, indeed they aren't.'

'Really,' said Diggory. 'I wish you'd speak the truth.'

With that he picked the second apple and threw it. And the old man began to speak the truth as hard as ever he could speak. It was like a child saying a lesson it has just learned, and is afraid of forgetting before it can get it said.

'I am a wicked magician. I have turned hundreds of people's heads in that tree so that they fall into the sky, and when they fall back again, as they have to do when the tide turns, I make them into apple-trees. I don't know why I do, but I like to. I suppose it's because I'm wicked. I never did anything useful with my magic, but I can hurt. And there's only one way out of this, and I don't mean to show it you.'

'It's a pity you're so wicked,' said Diggory. 'I wish you were good.'

He threw down another apple, and instantly the magician became so good that he could do nothing but sit down and cry to think how wicked he had been. He was now perfectly useless. But Diggory was no longer afraid of him,

so he gathered the ten apples that were left and put them inside his shirt, and came down the tree.

The old man couldn't tell him how to get out, and he couldn't disenchant the fruit-trees or anything. So Diggory had to spend three wish-apples. First he spent one on making the old man happy. This was done as it is in Miss Edgeworth's stories—by giving him a thatched cottage and a garden, and a devoted grand-daughter to look after him. The next apple showed Diggory the Apple Door, which he had not been able to find, and he went out by it. You, of course, can find it on the map, but he had no map, and besides, it is spelt differently. Before he went out of the orchard he threw down another apple, and wished the apple-trees to be disenchanted. And they were. And then the red-walled orchard was full of Kings and Princesses, and swineherds and goosegirls, and statesmen and steve-dores, and every kind of person you can or can't think of.

Diggory left them to find their own ways home—some of them lived ever so long before, and ever so far away—and he himself went out by the Apple Door, and found his good white horse, who had been eating grass very happily all the time he had been in the company of the magician, and that had been two days and a night.

So Invicta was not hungry, but Diggory was; and, in fact, he was so hungry that he had to use a wish-apple to get his supper, and that was very, very wasteful of him, and he often regretted it in after years. It is true that he wished for the best supper in the world, and had it; but it was only bread-and-milk! If he had wished for the nicest supper it would have been different, no doubt.

Diggory rode on anxiously, arranging what wishes he should have with the rest of the apples, but in the dusk he missed his way and was nearly drowned in a rain-flooded ford, and poor white Invicta was quite carried away.

Then Diggory took off his shirt to wring the water out, and as he took it off he said: 'I wish I had my good white horse again.'

And as he said it all the apples but one tumbled out of his shirt on to the ground, and he heard soft neighings and stampings and hustlings and rustlings all round him in the dark, and when the moon rose he saw that he had had his wish—he had his good white horse back again. But as he had dropped eight apples, he had his good white horse back eight times, and as eight times one is eight, he had now eight good white horses, all called Invicta.

'Well eight horses are better than nothing!' he said; and when he had tethered the horses he went to sleep, for he felt strangely feeble and tired.

In the morning he woke with pains in every limb. He thought it was a cold from the wetting in the ford, but it was really rheumatism. And he could not get rid of it. He tied seven horses together and led them, riding on the

eighth.

'Eight horses are a pretty good fortune for a wood-cutter's son,' he said to himself, 'and, anyway, I'm too tired to go looking for any better one.'

So he rode home.

He knew the roads well enough, and yet they seemed different; they were much better roads to ride over, for one thing, and the hedges and trees were odd somehow. And the big wood near his father's house seemed very small as he looked down on it from the hill. But when he got to the village he thought he must have gone mad, for in the day and two nights and a day that he had been away the village had grown big and ugly and yellow-bricky, and there were eight shops and six public-houses besides the Bill and Billet, and many more people than there used to be, all in ugly, untidy clothes, and the Round Mound windmill was *gone !* The people came crowding round him.

'What's become of the mill ?' he asked, trembling all over.

The boys and girls and men and women stared, and a very old man stepped out of the crowd.

'It were pulled down,' he said, 'when I were a boy.'

'And the woodcutter's cottage ?'

'That were burnt down a matter of fifty year ago. Was you a native of these parts, old man ?'

There was a large plate-glass shop-window just opposite the crowd that surrounded Diggory. A dark blind was pulled down inside, because it was Wednesday and early-closing day. This made a fine mirror, and Diggory happened to look in it, and there he saw himself—an old, old, white-haired man on a white horse. He had a white beard, too, but it was quite short, because it had only had since bedtime last night to grow in.

He almost tumbled off his horse. The landlord of the Ship led him in to sit by the fire in the bar parlour, and the eight horses were put up in the stable.

The old man who had told him about the mill came and sat by him, and poor old Diggory asked questions till he grew tired of hearing the answer, which was always the same: 'Dead, dead, dead!'

Then he sat silent, and the people in the bar talked about his horses, and a young man said:

'I wish I'd got e'er a one on 'em. I'd do a tidy bit in fish, an' set up for myself—so I would.'

'Young man,' said Diggory, 'you may take one of them; its name is Invicta.'

The young man could hardly believe his fortunate ears. Diggory felt his heart warm to think that he had made someone else so happy. He felt actually younger. And next morning he made up his mind to give away all the horses but one. That one he would sell, and its price would keep him for the rest of his life: he hoped that would not be long, for he did not care to go on living now that he had seen the tombstones in the churchyard with the names of his father and brothers and little Joyce of the mill.

He led his horses away next day. He did not want to give them all away in one village, because that would have lessened the value of his gift to the young man who was going into fish, and, besides, it would have been awkward to have so many horses of the same name in one village.

He gave away a horse at each village he passed through, and with every horse he gave away he felt happier and lighter. And when he had given away the fourth his rheumatism went, and when he had given away the seventh

his beard was gone.

'Now,' he said to himself, 'I will ride home and end my days in my own village, and be buried with my own people.'

So he turned his horse's head towards home, and he felt so gay and light-limbed he could hardly believe that he was really an old, old man. And he rode on.

And at the end of the village he stopped and rubbed his eyes, for there stood the Round Mound windmill, and on the slope was Joyce, looking prettier than ever in a russet petticoat and a white neckerchief and a pink print gown with little red rosebuds on it.

'Oh, Diggory, Diggory,' she cried, 'you've come back,

then! You'll take me with you now, won't you?'

'Have you got a looking-glass, my dear?' said he. 'Then run in and fetch it.'

She ran. He took it and looked in it. And he saw the same young brown face and the same bright brown hair that he had always known for *him*, and he was not old any more. And there was Joyce holding up a face as sweet as a bunch of flowers.

'Will you take me?' said she.

He stooped down and kissed the face that was so sweet.

'I'll take you,' said he.

And as they went along to his home he told her all the story.

'Well, but,' she said, 'you've got one wish-apple left.'

'Why, so I have,' said he; 'if I hadn't forgotten it!'

'We'll make that into the fortune you went out to find. Do, do let me look at it!'

He pulled out the apple, and she took it in her hand as she sat behind him on the big white horse.

'Yes, our fortune's made,' he said; 'but I do wish I knew why I turned old like that.'

Just then Invicta stumbled, and Joyce caught at her lover to save herself from falling, and as she caught at him the apple slipped from her hand and the last wish was granted. For as it bounced on the road Diggory did know why he had grown old like that. He knew that the magician had arranged long before that every wish-apple that was used outside the orchard should add ten years to the wisher's age. So that the eight horses had made him a hundred years old; and the spell could only be undone by the wisher's giving away what he's wished for. So that it was Diggory's generosity in giving away the horses that

had taken him back to the proper age for being happy in. I don't want to be moral, and I'm very sorry—but it really was that.

He carried Joyce home to his father's house. They were much too pleased with each other to bother about the wasted wish-apples.

'You're soon back, my son,' said the woodcutter, laughing.

'Yes,' said Diggory.

'Have you found your fortune?'

'Yes,' said Diggory; 'here she is!'

And he presented Joyce. The woodcutter laughed more than ever, for the miller's daughter was a bit of an heiress.

'Well, well!' he said.

So they were married, and they had a little farm, and the white horse was put to the plough, and to the cart,

and the harrow, and the waggon; and he worked hard,
and they worked hard, so that they all throve and were
very happy as long as ever they lived.

*   *   *

The only person in this story you are likely to have heard
of is, of course, Invicta, and he is better known as the
White Horse of Kent.

You can see pictures of him all over his county: on
brewers circulars and all sorts of documents, and carved in
stone on buildings, and even on the disagreeable, insulting
fronts of traction-engines. Traction-engines pretend to
despise horses, but they carry the image of the White
Horse on their hearts. And his name is generally put underneath his picture, so that there shall be no mistake.

Fortunatus Rex & Co.
or the Mystery of the Disappearing Schoolgirls

Fortunatus Rex & Co.
or
The Mystery of the Disappearing Schoolgirls

This refreshing story shows, once again, E. Nesbit's dashing mixture of ingredients old and new in the cauldron of her stories. Little schools, like Miss Fitzroy Robinson's, run in private houses, were plentiful in the late 18th and earlier 19th centuries; anyone who fancies a piece of exploring might see how many can be found in Dickens, for a start. And don't forget Mrs F. H. Burnett's *Sara Crewe* (or its longer version, *A Little Princess*). The Brontë sisters at one time thought of starting a school of their own in the Parsonage, and even made out a prospectus—but no one ever applied. Which was just as well. (Charlotte's last novel, called *Emma*, begun but never finished, was about a school of the kind.) A parlour boarder was a pupil who received special rather grown-up privileges (and paid more); such pupils were always valued. The globes, terrestrial (of the earth), celestial (of the sky), were a familiar part of such education. But if all this was old-fashioned even in E. Nesbit's time, speculative builders seem particularly modern. It is interesting that they were as much of a problem in E. Nesbit's day as now. In fact, they go a long way back in time. Sir Christopher Hatton was one in the 16th century, turning great orchards and gardens in Holborn into narrow city streets, which carry the old names to this day.

N.L.

THERE WAS ONCE a lady who found herself in middle life with but a slight income. Knowing herself to be insufficiently educated to be able to practise any other trade or calling, she of course decided, without hesitation, to enter the profession of teaching. She opened a very select Boarding School for Young Ladies. The highest references were given and required. And in order to keep her school as select as possible, Miss Fitzroy Robinson had a brass plate fastened on to the door, with an inscription in small polite lettering:

SELECT BOARDING ESTABLISHMENT FOR THE
DAUGHTERS OF RESPECTABLE MONARCHS

A great many kings who were not at all respectable would have given their royal ears to be allowed to send their daughters to this school, but Miss Fitzroy Robinson was very firm about references, and the consequence was that all the really high-class kings were only too pleased to be permitted to pay ten thousand pounds a year for their daughters' education. And so Miss Fitzroy Robinson was

127

able to lay aside a few pounds as a provision for her old age. And all the money she saved was invested in land.

Only one monarch refused to send his daughter to Miss Fitzroy Robinson, on the grounds that so cheap a school could not be a really select one, and it was found out afterwards that his references were not at all satisfactory.

There were only six boarders, and of course the best masters were engaged to teach the royal pupils everything which their parents wished them to learn, and as the girls were never asked to do lessons except when they felt quite inclined, they all said it was the nicest school in the world, and cried at the very thought of being taken away. Thus it happened that the six pupils were quite grown up and were just becoming parlour boarders when events began to occur. Princess Daisy, the daughter of King Fortunatus, the ruling sovereign, was the only *little* girl in the school.

Now it was when she had been at school about a year, that a ring came at the front door-bell, and the maid-servant came to the schoolroom with a visiting card held in the corner of her apron—for her hands were wet because it was washing-day.

'A gentleman to see you, Miss,' she said; and Miss Fitzroy Robinson was quite fluttered because she thought it might be a respectable monarch, with a daughter who wanted teaching.

But when she looked at the card she left off fluttering, and said, 'Dear me!' under her breath, because she was very genteel. If she had been vulgar like some of us she would have said 'Bother!' and if she had been more vulgar than, I hope, any of us are, she might have said 'Drat the man!' The card was large and shiny and had gold letters on it. Miss Fitzroy Robinson read:—

Chevalier Doloro De Lara
Professor of Magic (White)
and the Black Art.

Pupils instructed at their own residences.
No extras.

Special terms for Schools. Evening Parties
attended.

Miss Fitzroy Robinson laid down her book—she never taught without a book—smoothed her yellow cap and her grey curls and went into the front parlour to see her visitor. He bowed low at sight of her. He was very tall and hungry-looking, with black eyes, and an indescribable mouth.

'It is indeed a pleasure,' said he, smiling so as to show every one of his thirty-two teeth—a very polite, but very difficult thing to do—'it is indeed a pleasure to meet once more my old pupil.'

'The pleasure is mutual, I am sure,' said Miss Fitzroy Robinson. If it is sometimes impossible to be polite and truthful at the same moment, that is not my fault, nor Miss Fitzroy Robinson's.

'I have been travelling about,' said the Professor, still smiling immeasurably, 'increasing my stock of wisdom. Ah, dear lady—we live and learn, do we not ? And now I am really a far more competent teacher than when I had the honour of instructing you. May I hope for an engagement as Professor in your Academy ?'

'I have not yet been able to arrange for a regular course of Magic,' said the schoolmistress; 'it is a subject in which parents. especially royal ones, take but too little interest.'

'It was your favourite study,' said the professor.

'Yes—but—well, no doubt some day——'

'But I want an engagement *now*,' said he, looking hungrier than ever; 'a thousand pounds for thirteen lessons —to *you*, dear lady.'

'It's quite impossible,' said she, and she spoke firmly, for she knew from history how dangerous it is for a Magician to be allowed anywhere near a princess. Some harm almost always comes of it.

'Oh, very well!' said the Professor.

'You see my pupils are all princesses,' she went on, 'they don't require the use of magic, they can get all they want without it.'

'Then it's "*No*"?' said he.

'It's "No thank you kindly,"' said she.

Then, before she could stop him, he sprang past her out at the door, and she heard his boots on the oilcloth of the passage. She flew after him just in time to have the schoolroom door slammed and locked in her face.

'Well, I never!' said Miss Fitzroy Robinson. She hastened to the top of the house and hurried down the schoolroom chimney, which had been made with steps, in case of fire or other emergency. She stepped out of the grate on to the schoolroom hearthrug just one second too late. The seven Princesses were all gone, and the Pro-

fessor of Magic stood alone among the ink-stained desks, smiling the largest smile Miss Fitzroy Robinson had seen yet.

'Oh, you naughty, bad, wicked man, you!' said she, shaking the school ruler at him.

*　　*　　*

The next day was Saturday, and the King of the country called as usual to take his daughter Daisy out to spend her half holiday. The servant who opened the door had a coarse apron on and cinders in her hair, and the King thought it was sackcloth and ashes, and said so a little anxiously, but the girl said, 'No, I've only been a-doing of the kitchen range—though, for the matter of that—but you'd best see missus herself.'

So the King was shown into the best parlour where the tasteful wax-flowers were, and the antimacassars and water-colour drawings executed by the pupils, and the wool mats which Miss Fitzroy Robinson's bed-ridden aunt made so beautifully. A delightful parlour full of the traces of the refining touch of a woman's hand.

Miss Fitzroy Robinson came in slowly and sadly. Her gown was neatly made of sackcloth—with an ingenious trimming of small cinders sewn on gold braid—and some larger-sized cinders dangled by silken threads from the edge of her lace cap.

The King saw at once that she was annoyed about something. 'I hope I'm not too early,' said he.

'Your Majesty,' she answered, 'not at all. You are always punctual, as stated in your references. Something has happened. I will not aggravate your misfortunes by keeping them from you. Your daughter Daisy, the pride and treasure of our little circle, has disappeared. Her six royal companions are with her. For the present all are safe, but at the moment I am unable to lay my hand on any one of the seven.'

The King sat down heavily on part of the handsome walnut and rep suite (ladies' and gentlemen's easy-chairs, couch and six occasional chairs) and gasped miserably. He could not find words. But the schoolmistress had written down what she was going to say on a slate and learned it off by heart, so she was able to go on fluently.

'Your Majesty, I am not wholly to blame—hang me if I am—I mean hang me if you must; but first allow me to have the honour of offering to you one or two explanatory remarks.'

With this she sat down and told him the whole story of the Professor's visit, only stopping exactly where I stopped when I was telling it to you just now.

The King listened, plucking nervously at the fringe of a purple and crimson antimacassar.

'I never *was* satisfied with the Professor's methods,' said Miss Fitzroy Robinson sadly; 'and I always had my doubts as to his moral character, doubts now set at rest for ever. After concluding my course of instruction with him some years ago I took a series of lessons from a far more efficient master, and thanks to those lessons, which were, I may mention, extremely costly, I was mercifully enabled to put a spoke in the wheel of the unprincipled ruffian——'

'Did you save the Princesses?' cried the King.

'No; but I can, if your Majesty and the other parents will leave the matter entirely in my hands.'

'It's rather a serious matter,' said the King; 'my poor little Daisy——'

'I would ask you,' said the schoolmistress with dignity, 'not to attach too much importance to this event. Of course it is regrettable, but unpleasant accidents occur in all schools, and the consequences of them can usually be averted by the exercise of tact and judgment.'

'I ought to hang you, you know,' said the King doubtfully.

'No doubt,' said Miss Fitzroy Robinson, 'and if you do you'll never see your Daisy again. Your duty as a parent—yes—and your duty to me—conflicting duties are very painful things.'

'But can I trust you?'

'I may remind you,' said she, drawing herself up so that the cinders rattled again, 'that we exchanged satisfactory references at the commencement of our business relations.'

The King rose. 'Well, Miss Fitzroy Robinson,' he said, 'I have been entirely satisfied with Daisy's progress since she has been in your charge, and I feel I cannot do better than leave this matter entirely in your able hands.'

The schoolmistress made him a curtsey, and he went

back to his marble palace a broken-hearted monarch, with his crown all on one side and his poor nose red with weeping.

The select boarding establishment was shut up.

Time went on and no news came of the lost Princesses.

The King found but little comfort in the fact that his other child, Prince Denis, was still spared to him. Denis was all very well and a nice little boy in his way, but a boy is not a girl.

The Queen was much more broken-hearted than the King, but of course she had the housekeeping to see to and the making of the pickles and preserves and the young Prince's stockings to knit, so she had not much time for weeping, and after a year she said to the King—

'My dear, you ought to do something to distract your mind. It's unkinglike to sit and cry all day. Now, do make an effort; do something useful, if it's only opening a bazaar or laying a foundation stone.'

'I am frightened of bazaars,' said the King; 'they are like bees—they buzz and worry; but foundation stones ——' And after that he began to sit and think sometimes, without crying, and to make notes on the backs of old envelopes. So the Queen felt that she had not spoken quite in vain.

A month later the suggestion of foundation stones bore fruit.

The King floated a company, and Fortunatus Rex & Co. became almost at once the largest speculative builders in the world.

Perhaps you do not know what a speculative builder is. I'll tell you what the King and his Co. did, and then you will know.

They bought all the pretty woods and fields they could get and cut them up into squares, and grubbed up the trees and the grass and put streets there and lamp-posts and ugly little yellow brick houses, in the hopes that people would want to live in them. And curiously enough people did. So the King and his Co. made quite a lot of money.

It is curious that nearly all the great fortunes are made by turning beautiful things into ugly ones. Making beauty out of ugliness is very ill-paid work.

The ugly little streets crawled further and further out of the town, eating up the green country like greedy yellow caterpillars, but at the foot of the Clover Hill they had to stop. For the owner of Clover Hill would not sell any land at all—for any price that Fortunatus Rex & Co. could offer. In vain the solicitors of the Company called on the solicitors of the owner, wearing their best cloaks and swords and shields, and took them out to lunch and gave them nice things to eat and drink. Clover Hill was not for sale.

At last, however, a little old woman all in grey called at the Company's shining brass and mahogany offices and had a private interview with the King himself.

'I am the owner of Clover Hill,' said she, 'and you may build on all its acres except the seven at the top and the fifteen acres that go round that seven, and you must build me a high wall round the seven acres and another round the fifteen—of *red* brick, mind; none of your cheap yellow stuff—and you must make a brand new law that any one who steals my fruit is to be hanged from the tree he stole it from. That's all. What do you say?'

The King said 'Yes,' because since his trouble he cared for nothing but building, and his royal soul longed to see the green Clover Hill eaten up by yellow brick caterpillars with slate tops. He did not at all like building the two red walls, but he did it.

Now, the old woman wanted the walls and the acres to be this sort of shape—

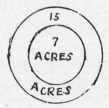

But it was such a bother getting the exact amount of ground into the two circles that all the surveyors tore out their hair by handfuls, and at last the King said, 'Oh bother! Do it this way,' and drew a plan on the back of an old Act of Parliament. So they did, and it was like this—

The old lady was very vexed when she found that there was only one wall between her orchard and the world, as you see was the case at the corner where the two 1's and the 15 meet; but the King said he couldn't afford to build it all over again and that she'd got her two walls as she had said. So she had to put up with it. Only she insisted on the King's getting her a fierce bull-dog to fly at the throat of any one who should come over the wall at that weak point where the two 1's join on to the 15. So he got her a stout bull-dog whose name was Martha, and brought it himself on a jewelled leash.

'Martha will fly at any one who is not of kingly blood,' said he. 'Of course she wouldn't dream of biting a royal person; but, then, on the other hand, royal people don't rob orchards.'

So the old woman had to be contented. She tied Martha up in the unprotected corner of her inner enclosure and then she planted little baby apple trees and had a house built and sat down in it and waited.

And the King was almost happy. The creepy, crawly yellow caterpillars ate up Clover Hill—all except the little green crown on the top, where the apple trees were and the two red brick walls and the little house and the old woman.

The poor Queen went on seeing to the jam and the pickles and the blanket washing and the spring cleaning, and every now and then she would say to her husband—

'Fortunatus, my love, do you *really* think Miss Fitzroy Robinson is trustworthy? Shall we ever see our Daisy again?'

And the King would rumple his fair hair with his hands till it stuck out like cheese straws under his crown, and

answer—

'My dear, you must be patient; you know we had the very highest references.'

Now one day, the new yellow brick town the King had built had a delightful experience. Six handsome Princes on beautiful white horses came riding through the dusty little streets. The housings of their chargers shone with silver embroidery and gleaming glowing jewels, and their gold armour flashed so gloriously in the sun that all the little children clapped their hands, and the Princes' faces were so young and kind and handsome that all the old women said: 'Bless their pretty hearts!'

Now, of course, you will not need to be told that these six Princes were looking for the six grown-up Princesses who had been so happy at the Select Boarding Establishment. Their six Royal fathers, who lived many years' journey away on the other side of the world, and had not yet heard that the Princesses were mislaid, had given Miss Fitzroy Robinson's address to these Princes, and instructed them to marry the six Princesses without delay, and bring them home.

But when they got to the Select Boarding Establishment for the Daughters of Respectable Monarchs, the house was closed, and a card was in the window, saying that this desirable villa residence was to be let on moderate terms, furnished or otherwise. The wax fruit under the glass

shade still showed attractively through the dusty panes. The six Princes looked through the window by turns. They were charmed with the furniture, and the refining touch of a woman's hand drew them like a magnet. They took the house, but they had their meals at the Palace by the King's special invitation.

King Fortunatus told the Princes the dreadful story of the disappearance of the entire Select School; and each Prince swore by his sword-hilt and his honour that he would find out the particular Princess that he was to marry, or perish in the attempt. For, of course, each Prince was to marry one Princess, mentioned by name in his instructions, and not one of the others.

The first night that the Princes spent in the furnished house passed quietly enough, so did the second and the third and the fourth, fifth and sixth, but on the seventh night, as the Princes sat playing spillikins in the schoolroom, they suddenly heard a voice that was not any of theirs. It said, 'Open up Africa!'

The Princes looked here, there, and everywhere—but they could see no one. They had not been brought up to the exploring trade, and could not have opened up Africa if they had wanted to.

'Or cut through the Isthmus of Panama,' said the voice again.

Now, as it happened, none of the six Princes were engineers. They confessed as much.

'Cut up China, then!' said the voice, desperately.

And then suddenly they knew that the voice came from one of the pair of globes which hung in frames at the end of the schoolroom. It was the terrestrial globe.

'I'm inside,' said the voice; 'I can't get out. Oh, cut the

globe—anywhere—and let me out. But the African route is most convenient.'

Prince Primus opened up Africa with his sword, and out tumbled half a Professor of Magic.

'My other half's in there,' he said, pointing to the Celestial globe. 'Let my legs out, do——'

But Prince Secundus said, 'Not so fast,' and Prince Tertius said, 'Why were you shut up?'

'I was shut up for as pretty a bit of parlour-magic as ever you saw in all your born days,' said the top half of the Professor of Magic.

'Oh, you were, were you?' said Prince Quartus; 'well, your legs aren't coming out just yet. We want to engage a competent magician. You'll do.'

'But I'm not all here,' said the Professor.

'Quite enough of you,' said Prince Quintus.

'Now look here,' said Prince Sextus; 'we want to find our six Princesses. We can give a very good guess as to how they were lost; but we'll let bygones be bygones. You tell us how to find them, and after our weddings we'll restore your legs to the light of day.'

'This half of me feels so faint,' said the half-Professor of Magic.

'What are we to do?' said all the Princes, threateningly; 'if you don't tell us, you shall never have a leg to stand on.'

'Steal apples,' said the half-Professor, hoarsely, and fainted away.

They left him lying on the bare boards between the ink-stained desks, and off they went to steal apples. But this was not so easy. Because Fortunatus Rex & Co. had built, and built, and built, and apples do not grow freely in those parts of the country which have been 'opened up' by speculative builders.

So at last they asked the little Prince Denis where he went for apples when he wanted them. And Denis said—

'The old woman at the top of Clover Hill has apples in her seven acres, and in her fifteen acres, but there's a fierce bulldog in the seven acres, and I've stolen all the apples in the fifteen acres myself.'

'We'll try the seven acres,' said the Princes.

'Very well,' said Denis; 'You'll be hanged if you're caught. So, as I put you up to it, I'm coming too, and if you won't take me, I'll tell. So there!'

For Denis was a most honourable little Prince, and felt that you must not send others into danger unless you go yourself, and he would never have stolen apples if it had not been quite as dangerous as leading armies.

So the Princes had to agree, and the very next night Denis let himself down out of his window by a knotted rope made of all the stockings his mother had knitted for him, and the grown-up Princes were waiting under the window, and off they all went to the orchard on the top of Clover Hill.

They climbed the wall at the proper corner, and Martha, the bulldog, who was very well-bred, and knew a

Prince when she saw one, wagged her kinked tail respect-
fully and wished them good luck.

The Princes stole over the dewy orchard grass and looked
at tree after tree: there were no apples on any of them.

Only at last, in the very middle of the orchard there was
a tree with a copper trunk and brass branches, and leaves
of silver. And on it hung seven beautiful golden apples.

So each Prince took one of the golden apples, very
quietly, and off they went, anxious to get back to the half-
Professor of Magic, and learn what to do next. No one had
any doubt as to the half-Professor having told the truth;
for when your legs depend on your speaking the truth you
will not willingly tell a falsehood.

They returned to the furnished house which had once
been a Select Boarding Establishment for the Daughters
of Respectable Monarchs and there, on the schoolroom
floor, lay half a Professor of Magic. He was struggling
feebly, and uttering sad, faint squeals.

'What are we to do now?' said Denis.

'Seven apples I tell you,' said the half-Professor, crossly.
'Orchards. Seven acres, seven apples—there—seven kisses.
Cut them down. Oh go along with you, do. Leave me to
die, you heartless boy. I've got pins and needles in my
legs.'

Off they ran to the Seven Acre Orchard at the top of
Clover Hill.

'Seven kisses!' cried, Denis, and began to kiss the little
golden apple which had been his choice.

Each Prince kissed the apple he held, till the sound of
kisses was like the whisper of the evening wind in leafy
trees. And, of course, at the seventh kiss each Prince found
that he had in his hand not an apple, but the fingers of a

lovely Princess. As for Denis, he had got his little sister Daisy, and he was so glad he promised at once to give her his guinea-pigs and his whole collection of foreign postage stamps.

'What is your name, dear and lovely lady?' asked Prince Primus.

'Sexta,' said his Princess. And then it turned out that every one of the Princes had picked the wrong apple, so that each one had a Princess who was not the one mentioned in his letter of instructions. Secundus had plucked the apple that held Quinta, and Tertius held Quarta, and so on—and everything was as criss-cross-crooked as it possibly could be.

And yet nobody wanted to change.

Then the old woman came out of her house and looked at them and chuckled, and she said—

'You must be contented with what you have.'

'We *are*,' said all twelve of them, 'but what about our parents?'

'They must put up with your choice,' said the old woman, 'it's the common lot of parents.'

'I think you ought to sort yourselves out properly,' said Denis; 'I'm the only one who's got his right Princess—because I wasn't greedy. I took the smallest.'

But the old woman said—

'They can't change, my dear. When a Prince has picked a gold apple that has a Princess in it, and has kissed it till she comes out, no other Princess will ever do for him, any more than any other Prince will ever do for her.'

While she was speaking the old woman got younger and younger and younger, till as she spoke the last words she was quite young, not more than fifty-five. And it was Miss

Fitzroy Robinson!

Her pupils stepped forward one by one with respectful curtsies, and she allowed them to kiss her on the cheek, just as if it was breaking-up day.

Then, all together, and very happily, they went down to the furnished villa that had once been the Select School, and when the half-Professor had promised on his honour as a Magician to give up Magic and take to a respectable trade, they took his legs out of the starry sphere, and gave them back to him; and he joined himself together, and went off full of earnest resolve to live and die an honest plumber.

'My talents won't be quite wasted,' said he; 'a little hanky-panky is useful in most trades.'

When the King asked Miss Fitzroy Robinson to name her own reward for restoring the Princesses, she said—

'Make the land green again, your Majesty.'

So Fortunatus Rex & Co. devoted themselves to pulling down and carting off the yellow streets they had built. And now the country there is almost as green and pretty as it was before Princess Daisy and the six parlour-boarders were turned into gold apples.

'It was very clever of dear Miss Fitzroy Robinson to shut up that Professor in those two globes,' said the Queen; 'it shows the advantage of having lessons from the *best* Masters.'

'Yes,' said the King, 'I always say that you cannot go far wrong if you insist on the highest references!'